MW00324395

"This book was written by George Benet in the early 50's. Benet stopped writing until the early 70's when he began to publish under his own name. His other books are *A Place in Colusa* and *A Short Dance in the Sun*. ... *The Hoodlums* is not only an enjoyable read, but easily the best thing Benet ever wrote."

—*GoodReads*

"George Benet has brought the 'real novel' out of the perfumed garbage pail and returned it to its rightful place in American writing."

—Leonard Bishop, *The Manhattan Mercury*

"As a writer, he has been proclaimed as Marxists to be an authentic voice of the proletariat ..."

—Mickey Friedman,
Sunday Examiner & Chronicle

HOODLUMS

Published by Black Gat Books
A division of Stark House Press
1315 H Street
Eureka, CA 95501, USA
griffinskye3@sbcglobal.net
www.starkhousepress.com

HOODLUMS
Originally published in paperback by Avon Books, New York, and copyright
© 1953 by John Eagle.

Copyright © 2021 by Stark House Press. All rights reserved under
International and Pan-American Copyright Conventions.

ISBN-13: 978-1-951473-23-5

Book design by Jeff Vorzimmer, ¡caliente!design, Austin, Texas
Proofreading by Bill Kelly
Cover art by Kirk Wilson from the original Avon edition.

PUBLISHER'S NOTE:
This is a work of fiction. Names, characters, places and incidents are either
the products of the author's imagination or used fictionally, and any
resemblance to actual persons, living or dead, events or locales, is entirely
coincidental.

Without limiting the rights under copyright reserved above, no part of this
publication may be reproduced, stored, or introduced into a retrieval system
or transmitted in any form or by any means (electronic, mechanical,
photocopying, recording or otherwise) without the prior written permission
of both the copyright owner and the above publisher of the book.

First Stark House Press/Black Gat Edition: February 2021

George Benet Bibliography
(1918-1990)

As by John Eagle
The Hoodlums (1953)

As by George Benet
A Place in Colusa (1977; stories & poems)
A Short Dance in the Sun (1988)

HOODLUMS

by George Benet
writing as
John Eagle

Black Gat Books • Eureka California

CHAPTER I

The straight razor scraped along the stubble. Kirk Wagner looked into the mirror. His face, under the blond crewcut hair, was tanned. The razor moved at different angles over the square jaw, cutting into the lather. He scooped cold water on his face. Now the towel.

Carefully Kirk cleaned the razor. It had been a gift from his mother before her death. He turned the blade in his hand with fascination. Expensive. He rubbed his finger on the trademark. J. A. Henckels, Twinworks, Solingen, Germany. Two trademark figures showed dark against the blue steel. Steel as blue as his eyes, he thought. He balanced the ivory handle and blade on one finger. With one stroke the blade moved along his arm, for one inch it cleared hair and left a path.

His tall, powerful figure bent slightly as the long thickly muscled arms easily stropped the blade over the leather.

Kirk moved down the hall toward his room. Barney had always said he was lucky, smart and aggressive. Why was he flat on his can? Without money, without a car, barely able to scrape four dollars for the meeting with Jeannie today. He had held a job for two days. But the time clock, the punching in every morning, then eight hours at one bench, hunched over one lathe had been too much. He had taken a chance before, and the three long years in prison had canceled that debt. In his heart Kirk knew he would take a chance again. The world was a house of angles. You had to grab one in your teeth, hang on, ride it out. Some day end up on top of

the heap. And when you were young. No use
grabbing the gold ring off the merry-go-round when
you were sixty years old and wrinkled. No use spending money for nurses, wheelchairs, and drugs. Hit it
hard when the chance came, and maybe with some
luck he would lay up with some broad like Jeannie.
Kirk imagined the soft flesh in his palms, and the
burnt-cork taste of good whisky swooshing past his
tongue. Pushing the bathing suit into his pocket, he
walked out the door.

Outside, the sun scorched the street and steam
hissed from the asphalt. Kirk's long arms lowered and
the thick, heavy fingers held the dirty rag doll lying
on the sidewalk. In the background, pushing against
his thoughts, he heard the thuds and occasional clang
of the horseshoes from the next-door lot. Touching
the grilled fence made his fingers jump from the iron
as if it were electric. Then carefully, Kirk placed the
rag doll on the top step, off to the side where no one
could kick it accidentally.

Kirk's energetic steps led into the July Sunday
buzz of Sixty-third Street. He noticed the grimy
buildings the color of dirty water, and the crowded,
noisy street with its claptrap elevated. Excited voices
from a sleek convertible irritated him. His nostrils
twitched from the spirals of the car's exhaust. This
was the end of a dream. The end product of a
thousand lamented nights. Three years in prison for
the gun beef. Three years of anguish over Martin's
doublecross and escape with the money. The violence
of what he might do to Martin only interrupted by
the restlessness of the deep, round prison darkness
that had carried him dream after dream into the soft
arms of Jeannie with her nipples pink as a white
rabbit's eye. Kirk tried to fit the images. Prison only
two weeks removed, and here was Chicago

shimmering in the yellow glow as if a Bessemer converter lay below the asphalt.

Braced against Metzner's window, he watched Jeannie emerge from the shadow of the Illinois Central viaduct. This was a new Jeannie. Not the one he had tussled with on the decks of the *Santa Maria*, the replica of one of Columbus's ships at the north end of the Jackson Park lagoon. He had come close, but close is only good in horseshoes. She had been seventeen then, but the taller, fuller-shaped Jeannie that approached shouted an improvement.

From the obscene wiggle of her bare toes held by the leather strips of open sandals, to the thick rolls of dark-brown hair cascading to her slim, erect shoulders, Jeannie had changed. The leggy girlish walk had dissolved into a jungle cat's velvety glide. Kirk shuddered and checked himself from touching the baby-pink flesh that pressed taut against white shorts and sheer blouse.

"Good morning, Kirk. Or is it afternoon?" Jeannie shielded her eyes and the dimples showed. She held a pair of sun-glasses in her right hand. A shoulder purse swung by her side.

"Where are we going?"

"Fifty-ninth Street beach." She adjusted the sun-glasses to her eyes. "You've been gone a long time, Kirk. We should celebrate your return."

He offered her his arm. "We can have a cool drink later."

The lascivious way her tongue wet the thick lips, and the heavy swells in her blouse caused Kirk's hands to sweat. They walked across the street to Jackson Park.

"There's Christine's blanket," Kirk said. Jeannie fell to her knees on the blanket. Kirk laid his slacks

down at the edge. He had put on his suit in the
washhouse. They sat knees up facing the water.

"Isn't the sun glorious? No wonder everyone's
out," Jeannie's voice was husky, resonant, almost
barrelhouse. Kirk looked down the beach. Some
yellow-and-blue umbrellas were to the left; and over
his shoulder he could see the weight-lifting crowd. He
knew some of them. They were all tan and their
muscles bulged as they grunted. One kid's back was
an abnormal triangle. Big shoulders and rippling back
carried by thin bony legs. He remembered his one
argument at the "Y" with one of these burly boys, as
they were called. The man was built like a box. It had
started in the pool and ended in the alley. Three
punches and the boxlike figure had been stretched
with his head cocked on a telephone pole. A weight
lifter was like a bear, grab and crush. Kirk had a
theory on that. A fast straight puncher could make
breakfast out of them all day. He dug his hand into
the sand.

Jeannie turned her head back. "Grotesque, aren't
they?" One thing about Jeannie, he had always
noticed. She wasn't a flirt in public.

Down the beach he could see the red jerseyed
lifeguards run a boat out, jump in, grab the paddles.
People were diving from the pilings of the broken pier
to the right. Jeannie had her blouse and shorts off.
Her two-piece bathing suit was spotted like a leopard,
and it didn't leave much to the imagination. She had
it. Jeannie took some suntan oil from the bag. She
rolled on her stomach and held the bottle back to
Kirk.

"Put some on."

Kirk applied the oil gently. From the corner of his
eye he could see Doyle, a man about forty, who wore
big glasses under a cap; and always winter or summer

a gray jersey sweater. Kirk watched the peaked, pontifical face. Behind the face was a complicated mind. Kirk had heard him quote everything from diamond cutting to the glacial ages. Doyle could name the streets of Hippias in numerical order, or give the nomenclature of a milling machine. It was hard for Kirk to evaluate Doyle, as hard as it was to evaluate anyone who didn't fit the neighborhood's mold. Oblivious to money and content to wrap his body in soiled and dirty clothes, the closest Doyle came to being a steady member of any group was the fluid, Sterno gang, ruled by the hatchet-faced Big Gump. Unlike Gump, who moved along the razor edge of violence and brutality, Doyle even in the ragbag clothes had a sort of pristine chasteness. Kirk centered on the weak chin. Kirk waved, only to miss recognition as Doyle turned his head.

Kirk's fingers tingled when he touched the baby-pink flesh.

"Am I rubbing too hard?" he asked Jeannie.

"Rub along the side." Her arms were over her head and his finger slipped along the edge of her breasts which were pressed out under her weight.

"Not there."

Jeannie's satiny skin was warm and moist to his touch. A tingling following the fingers as they kneaded the shoulders and trailed along the ridges of the spine to end at the fully cushiony hips. The warm skin oozed a promise of things to come. Kirk trembled, became nervous inside. The desire to carry Jeannie across the drive into one of the park's deep glades became dominant. His mind formed primitive patterns.

"Hey, look who's here, Chris. Bullethead." Jake's halfback frame stood over Jeannie. The round face wobbled from side to side, and drops of water from

the shining black curly hair made globules on
Jeannie's oiled back. Christine, a slender dishwater
blonde, was beside him. With legs slightly bowed she
stood pensive. When this slight girl smiled, Kirk knew
a broken tooth would show.... "Who's the leopard
with you?" Jake asked.

"Don't be funny," said Jeannie raising herself to a
sitting position.

"We're going for a walk," Christine said.

"No, thank you," Jeannie answered.

"Do you want anything from the shack?" asked
Jake.

"Bring us some coke," said Kirk. He reached for
his slacks.

"I got it, big shot," Jake said, patting his change
pocket in his suit.

When Jake and Christine left, Kirk asked, "Going
in for a swim?"

"Later."

Kirk watched Jeannie comb her loose hair. A mass
of dark-brown hair fell across her eye—thick and
massed, like the animal underbrush of the primeval
forest.

"Did you know I have a new job?" Jeannie said.

"At the 'Idle Hour'."

"No, since then. In fact, I didn't get it until last
month." Her fingers were on his arm. "This is the
break I have been waiting for. Two men came down
to the 'Idle Hour' to see the show. One man heads a
modeling agency. He knew the manager and saw my
strip from the wings.... You knew I did the headline
strip at the 'Idle Hour'."

"Barney mentioned it to me."

"So the head of this agency liked my style. A
meeting was arranged. We went out after the show.
The next night I quit the 'Idle Hour'. Easy."

"What do you model?"

"Everything, but mostly for a camera. Some nights before a camera. Some nights for a photography class."

"You mean without clothes?"

"For twenty-five dollars an hour, I'd model inside out."

"Twenty-five dollars per is big money for an ordinary model."

"Maybe they are grooming me for a trip to Hollywood."

"Maybe," said Kirk.

Jeannie squinted her nose in the sun. He stood up, grabbed her hand but it was limp.

"Coming?"

"Not now, Kirk. You go in. I'll join you on the second trip."

He ran to the water, splashing everyone who stood in the shallow part. A quick crawl stroke carried him out to the deep. His toes dangled but he could not touch bottom. He made a short dive and with hands in a breast stroke, his chest skirted along the sand. In the dim green he saw legs kicking. His eyes picked out the rocks and small dark spots that dotted the sand. When his breath was out, he zoomed to the surface and filled his lungs with oxygen. He paddled around. Looking back to the beach, he moved his head until he saw Jeannie. She was still alone and reading something she held in her hand. Treading water momentarily, he wondered about Jeannie's concentration.

The water was clear and blue out in the deep. A beach ball was moving into the current. No one was near. Kirk calculated the ball and the angle. His arms leaped forward. With easy strokes he moved to cut off the ball. When the ball moved faster, bouncing slightly on the waves from a small wind, Kirk moved faster. The ball was past him and he was behind trying to catch it. Elusive and easy to misjudge. He thought, like Jeannie. His legs whipped the water in a flutter kick. Arms dipping in and out. He was gaining but his breath was shortening. He caught the ball near the bend at the Fifty-fifth Street rocks. Resting on the ball, holding on, Kirk regained his wind. With the small beach ball under one arm and moving the other side stroke, he worked the ball into the cove at Fifty-third Street. Shielded from the current he made strokes to a ladder. He balanced the ball and stepped onto the rocks. People were sitting on blankets and some were diving, doing swans and jackknifes from the high ledges. He picked his way through the hot rocks and across the sand. Once on the grass, his feet felt better. He walked back to the Fifty-ninth Street beach.

Jake and Christine were back. Jeannie held a coke which she handed to him.

"I watched you," she said.

"Rough, wasn't it?" asked Jake.

"I knew I'd get it."

"You're persistent when you want to be," Jeannie said.

Kirk searched his shirt for the lone cigar. He had a feeling Jeannie was watching him, measuring him.

"I do have possibilities," he said, inhaling the warm smoke, feeling it creep into the crevices of his lungs.

"So did Dempsey," said Jake, who threw his arm over Christine as they lay face down.

Kirk puffed on the cigar, and Jeannie waited until he was finished before she asked, "Do you feel like going in again?"

"Sure. Any time."

They walked to the water's edge, and Kirk knew many eyes were on the scanty leopard suit. Jeannie moved slowly into the water, but she waited a moment at the edge. "Don't splash my hair," she said,

"Aren't you going in?" he asked.

"Yes. But not all the way."

"Why didn't you wear a hat?"

"I can't swim anyway," she said as he stood next to her in the water at their knees. "Don't duck me."

"I won't."

Her hand was in his and they moved out farther.

They were at hip length. "Do you want me to show you how to swim?"

"If you don't duck me."

Kirk balanced her. Jeannie splashed her arms and her feet slipped back to the sand.

"You'll have to hold me up better."

"Wait, let's get away from the crowd." He guided her to a spot where the water was waist deep. "Now don't worry."

He held her again. Tighter this time and her body squirmed. Kirk's hand held at her chest and the fullness of her breasts squashed against his palm. She straightened up. "Was I better that time?"

He dipped down to his shoulder.

"Again," she said.

This time he held her firm. And she floated on the top. His left hand moved along her thigh. Her legs were moving.

Her flesh fitted in his palm. Jeannie said nothing but floated lazily. Her legs dropped back to the sand.

"Having fun?" She smiled, splashing water at his eyes. How different she was. More receptive than she had ever been.

"You seem different today."

"Perhaps, because you're not used to women."

"No, something else."

He had his hands on her waist, her hands on his shoulder bouncing her in the water.

"Do you ever lose your suit when you dive?" she asked.

"Sometimes."

"Isn't it funny?"

"No one knows. I put it on again."

Her back was against his chest. She floated away. His hand caught the bow of her top and it came loose.

"Oops." She caught the front that floated on the surface. "Will you tie it, Kirk?"

The water came up to Jeannie's shoulders. Kirk moved his hands to cup her breasts. She rested her head back and her hair brushed his cheek and lips.

"We better go in," she said.

Kirk was in the washhouse changing from his suit to slacks when Jake entered.

"How you doing, Kirk?" Jake asked. His flushed, red face broke into sun wrinkles when he squinted, the eyes becoming small slits.

"Wonderful to be back. Jeannie's next door."

"Are you trying to pick up where you left off? Jeannie's in the big leagues. She hasn't dated anyone from the neighborhood."

"What about Martin?"

"No word since he left for St. Louis. And that was only a few days before you went up the river." Jake twisted his suit dry. "This is the last swim for me this summer."

"How come?"

"School. I'm going to Illinois Wesleyan next week. Have a job on a farm to work off this fat for football season." Jake gripped the excess roll around his middle. "You know, Kirk. You had a year at Tulane. Why not go back? Hell, you're in trim. Maybe you can make the team."

"At twenty-six? I'm an old man. There's only one thing to set me right. The jack. The moola."

"That's Martin's line. Don't get mixed up with that character again."

"He's not here," Kirk said.

"He will be. His kind always come back. Sixty-third's not a neighborhood for his kind. It's a disease.... See you, Kirk. Chris is waiting in the car. Want a lift?"

"We'll walk."

Jake's stocky figure moved out into the sunlight. Funny thing about Jake, Kirk thought. His simple aspirations violated every concept of Kirk's idea of success. Simple aspirations as a physical education major would put him on some high school staff. Kirk shook his head at the thought.

Doyle had entered. He looked seedy. Kirk thought of Prohibition and Clara Bow as the symbol of the filled silk stockings, and the perfectly round legs. This was Doyle's generation. Something distant and old. There was a chasm between them. Doyle must be in his late forties, he gauged. Twenty years of peering into books had given Doyle's eyes an exaggerated brightness like a funhouse mirror. Doyle's concupiscent lips twitched.

"It's good to see you, Kirk." He offered a hand soft as a dead fish. "Are you alone?"

"Jeannie's next door." He watched Doyle's lips tighten. Then with jerky movements Doyle left. What a queer duck, Kirk said to himself. Then inwardly he tried to retract the thought. Why should he think these people were all different? He thought of his three years out of circulation. Three years of tin plates and the hard grifter faces. Who is different, he questioned himself. They were all from the same mold. Even Martin. Martin's name crossing his memory caused him to wrench the suit viciously. He walked out the door.

Jeannie leaned against the white wall of the washhouse. With the suit off he could see the ridges of her nipples in the sweater.

She acknowledged his look. "We better walk along some less congested parts."

"I thought you were a model," he joked, focusing his hands like a camera.

"I don't get paid here. Besides some of the old ladies won't understand. I forgot to bring a brassiere." Her arm went through his and when traffic stopped for a red light, they ran across the street. He took her along the path that followed the lagoon.

When they neared Stony Island, Jeannie said, "We can walk down Sixty-second."

"How about a tall cool one?"

Her hands were on her hips, the white shoulder-purse-lay along her thigh. Kirk could see she was thinking.

"Can we have one at my place? Have you any money for some mix?" Jeannie asked.

Kirk showed her the small roll.

Kirk looked over Jeannie's place while she changed in the bedroom. Nice spot for a lone girl, he thought. The curtain drifted around the sill, outside the window a big elm rustled in the new breeze. In the bathroom he saw a razor perched on the cabinet, and his mind went back to the water and her flesh. He heard Jeannie moving in the kitchen.

The drinks were ready and outside the sun was

fading. The long shadows made the room dim. She had turned on the radio. Jeannie sat on the lone armchair. She wore a housecoat with small insect patterns, black and gold on the white coat. She had furry mules on her feet. The drink was cool. Kirk mixed the next, allowed the whisky to run and gurgle in the glass.

"Don't get drunk."

"I won't," he answered.

He took a sip and walked over to Jeannie pulling her to her feet. His mouth found hers. She certainly has improved, Kirk said to himself, thinking back to the *Santa Maria*. Her eyelash tickled his cheek and he could feel her breasts rub against him. By now the sun was down, and the street lights were on. He gripped Jeannie hard again. With one hand he opened the belt, and the housecoat fell to the floor. In the dim light he could see she had nothing on. Her body arched backward. The glimmering sheen of flesh shot desire into his veins. He pulled her hips until they pressed tantalizingly against his. Her breath, hot as a steel furnace, fanned his neck.

The door-buzzer sounded, shattering the stillness of the room. Jeannie gathered the housecoat, quickly retied the belt.

"Kirk, you have to go."

"Why? Who is it?"

"My boss." Jeannie paused and the buzzer sounded again. "I forgot that he was coming so soon." Kirk knew she was lying. Not about it being her boss, but about him being expected. Kirk stalled.

"Go, Kirk," she coaxed.

"Can't you ditch him?"

"Mr. Otis would fire me."

"So it was Mr. Otis now."

"Please go." Jeannie pushed him toward the door.

The buzzer went off again. "Here's a kiss."

Kirk held her close. He was planning, Jeannie was in a spot.

"Can I see you again?"

"Yes. Yes. Now go."

"When."

"Any time."

"Next Saturday at the Casino?"

"Yes."

"What time should I call?"

"Don't call here. I'll meet you there at ten."

She had Kirk out in the hall. "Go down the back way. Please."

"Next Saturday," he reminded her.

"Yes," and the white door closed.

She would be talking on the communication phone. And the buzzer at the front door would let Mr. Otis in. A good thing for Jeannie that the apartment house had a locked front door, he thought. Kirk walked down the back stairs and the exit brought him to the alley. He had come close tonight. Unusually close for Jeannie. Maybe his luck was changing. Somehow he tried to figure the difference in Jeannie tonight.

Unsatisfied, Kirk waited in the building's passageway. Fifteen long minutes ticked by before Jeannie's legs moved toward the curb. A filmy, pink, chiffon dress floated with her pelvis slack. There was enough rhythm in her walk to raise King Tut's blood pressure. A short perspiring fat man hurried to walk beside her. She bent low to enter the tan new Lincoln. Kirk heard her throaty laughter and all that was left in the fading light was a flickering red taillight. "That babe is moving into class," he said half aloud, his mouth dry.

The night air had washed the city with a flavor of witches' brew, and Sixty-third and Stony was teeming. A hook-and-ladder clattered up the street. Kirk wondered if some drunk had fallen asleep with a lit cigarette. The traffic resumed, and he picked his way nimbly past the sprawled drunks, avoiding the handout artists. He visualized the morning paper. On the back pages at least one bottled to death in a dismal passageway. Christ, he thought, the only difference between the older man in the roadster and these drunks of Muscatel Alley was money. Rest your head on two pillow breasts or rot on the hard cement. Where would he be at fifty? The shadow of himself fell into step behind him. Someone was whistling, *Me and My Shadow*. Kirk walked faster.

A man on rubbery legs danced crazily in front of the plate-glass window. The froggy voices of the bums croaked in Kirk's head, as he entered the beery smelling bar, wading through the beer-filled air, Kirk paused to watch the vague shapes in pantomime assembled between the atabrine-colored walls. The bar was one of five on the corner of Sixty-third and Stony. All five were connected by a back passageway. Kirk knew this passageway served three functions: To keep the drunks from getting lost in the vast outside world. They could wander from place to place unseen by the street people. Also after hours with the shades down they could move between the places unmolested by the law. Kirk recognized that this was a flimsy conjecture never put to the test. He believed these places would never be molested by the law, unless by a rookie cop unfamiliar with the machine party caucuses or the symbiotic relation between tavern owners, ward committeemen and police captains. But it kept the more grotesque and dilapidated drunks away from the reformers' eyes, and also kept them out of the cold. Kirk could hear Barney the newsboy cynic saying, "If somebody shot fifty of the drunks around Sixty-third, the bars who were up to their ass in mortgages would close."

Kirk glanced at the bar-shapes, reshuffling them in his memory. Most were oldtimers, except Jake, who was standing, one foot on the rail, a beer poised in his hand. Jake's flat nose crinkled and the small eyes squinted.

"What'll you have?" he asked.

Kirk ordered a shot and seltzer.

"Jeannie forgot something."

"What?"

Jake extended a flat thick letter. No return address on it. Just Jeannie's name and address.

"You can give this to her. Can't you, Kirk?"

"Sure, pal, sure." Kirk bought Jake another beer. "You and Chris getting on?"

"She's talking marriage." Jake shook his head. "I don't know, Kirk."

"Good kid, Christine."

"The best," Jake said. They drank a toast.

At home later in the room with the lights on, Kirk sat in the rocking chair. The swim-suit on the floor.

He turned the flat envelope in his hand. The writing of the name and address was in a fine hand, and the green ink interested Kirk. He played with the idea, and when the sheets were out, he looked at the last page. Page twenty-three. What a long-winded bastard, he muttered. And when his eyes started, they didn't stop until the last page. Dear Jeannie Cartier, it started. And from there on. Kirk shook his head. He had never read a letter like this. Almost like the graybook French Secretary's story, only worse. More imagination. The writer knew Jeannie or had seen her without clothes. He knew Jeannie's actions, way of

walking, facial expressions. The letter was written as
a dream. She was dressed fancy. A lot of details in
describing the clothes. On the third page the clothes
were gone! Negroes beating drums, wild dances
almost like a marijuana jag. That's it, thought Kirk, a
marijuana jag. No sober person could write this. In
the rest, every sexual position in the book and in
delicate details. The writing was smooth, even,
unbroken. And Kirk sensed that others had preceded
this letter and more would follow. Only one thing set
this off: the writer didn't leave his name, he was
unknown to Jeannie.

Kirk looked at the date on the envelope. The letter
was dated six days ago. Mailed from a Hyde Park
mailbox. Why did Jeannie have it today? He
remembered Jeannie reading something at the beach.
He guessed many crackpots sent letters to strippers
and movie stars; he imagined that they burned them
or turned them over to the police. What was Jeannie
doing with the letter six days after mailing? He was
sober now and his mind tried to fit the parts. Maybe
she had gone down for the letter today. Everything
jumbled. He looked at the clock, four in the morning.
Kirk reread the last ten pages. He was baffled by the
vivid description and imagination. In a funny way
Kirk felt that Jeannie could do these things. That
would be a way to get at Jeannie. As the writer said,
her love of nice things, silks, jade meant that she was
a sybarite. Kirk reminded himself to look up the word
tomorrow.

He lay in bed and tossed. A new worry had come
up. Had Christine read it? No, she wouldn't. Another
problem. What to do with it. Throw it away? Return
it to Jeannie. She would know he had read it. He
wouldn't be able to keep a straight face.

He lay in bed and tried to avoid thinking about

the letter. His mind jumbled: Martin's doublecross and disappearance, Jeannie purring like a cat, a soft Persian with smoldering, brown eyes, and the buildings of the city melting down like chocolate dissolving into a high-tree jungle. The cats are out, he cautioned himself. He tossed around, and at five when the gray edges of dawn rolled across the flat rooftops and the garbage men clanked their battered cans, Kirk moved into a deep sleep.

CHAPTER II

Kirk's head lay on the pillow and the evening air settled into the shadowed corners. In the distance he could hear the intermittent rattle of the elevated trains. By the luminous hands on the clock, it was almost time to meet Big Gump. In this quiet hour between the flushed spastic heat of day and the neon glamour of night, Kirk had his peace. The time of retracing, a time devoid of the decibels of noise when piano wires of the past came in with the shadows, crowded the room with yesterday's night songs. He sentimentalized on his mother, remembering her stories about old Chicago. She had always remarked at how the city was changing. Her plans about going West, out where the sun shone all the year round, no sleet or November wind. Kirk had known for years that his mother had been a dreamer, a chaser of catalogs, a looker at maps. Just leave. She was always leaving. Just like the night she had seen the newsreel about Rio de Janeiro. She had had him get photographs from the library. Look at the pictures. Imagine herself at the Rio shops. Yet she had never escaped further than a hundred miles from Chicago. A temporary escape, yes. Walk from the grimy city,

leave the smelly garbage smell of the city. Part
temporarily from the million house jobs so stifling to
every housewife. Escape yes, sometimes on Sunday in
the summer to the park. Go to the Japanese houses on
Wooded Island or take a ride with the old man to
Western Avenue. Buy some watermelons but always
back to the cracked plaster walls and the shared
bathroom. No marble or mango groves. And he could
sense in himself the same restlessness instilled from
the distant past from the barbaric German races. The
sackers of Rome, the wanderers in the Rhineland. But
now the city could grind a person's guts into a finely
labeled powder called futility; and Kirk knew
something deep inside what his mother had never
known. There was no escape, the concrete blocks
from the Loop to Gary were a lost maze, and the
small exits were only temporary.

Arching his back he pulled the lone one-dollar bill
from his pocket. Christ, he thought, Big Gump and I
better connect tonight or he would never make the
dance. He rose from the davenport, washed his face
quickly. Stretching to his five foot eleven, Kirk felt his
back muscles tighten. He pulled the long arms out
and back in mock exercise, finally bringing the hands
together, to end by cracking the bony knuckles one by
one. In the mirror his blue eyes were cold as Alaric's
steel. His reading habits and the love of history he
had acquired in the short time at Tulane came back to
haunt him. His eyes hadn't been this hard then; but
neither had times been this tough. He remembered
Gump, and with deft fingers he dressed in his darkest
clothes.

Outside, the evening was as empty as an
undertaker's heart, and his long legs carried him
down Stony Island toward the Sixty-third Street park
entrance. The hard-steel, late-afternoon sky had

faded, and the night air rustled the park's trees. Over to the southeast the East Chicago steel mills sent up a barbaric orange glow.

He found Big Gump sitting on the second bench near the elevated station rolling a cigarette from a crumpled Bull Durham pack.

"How's things look, Gump?" Kirk asked in a friendly tone.

"Good pickin's," answered Big Gump, raising his six foot five inch gangling frame from the bench, then placing one monstrous shoe on the bench. Kirk was seated and watching Gump's easy jaw clicking under the seedy cap. Gump was thin through the shoulders but the entire body exuded power and energy. The many years of gandy dancing for the railroad had polished the lean frame with a shell of stringy muscle. Gump would make a tough enemy, Kirk surmised.

They made their plans and then entered the park. Big Gump was to go to the bushes that rimmed the old football field. He would stay behind a tree ten feet from the bench. From his spot he would see the big cube.... The Hotel Plaisance rising behind him. Kirk took the gravel path called Maiden Lane and seated himself on an opportune bench. Sooner or later he would be approached by one of the many marks that lingered at this particular spot in the park.

The approach was usual this night. The fellow who sat next to Kirk wore a sport coat. He offered a cigarette and followed with the customary line.

"What's a young fellow like you doing in the park all alone on a Saturday night?" asked the mark.

Kirk lit his cigarette, cupping his hand around the match and extinguishing it quickly, careful not to show his face too long in the dark area. "Broke and no place to go, I guess," answered Kirk diplomatically, allowing the smoke to exude with the words. He puffed in silence leaving the lead to the other person. He had to be sure this wasn't one of the many detectives that hung around the park. Usually easy to pick out the new imports.

"Why aren't you out with your girl friend?"

"Too much trouble," stated Kirk, giving the desired answer. "All they want is someone with a lot of jack."

They kept up this cat-and-mouse game until the mark was satisfied; and then he made his pass. The hand on the bicep type, the more cautious kind, "You're husky. Did you ever do any boxing?"

"Never, just plenty of hard work." Kirk saw the deep-shadowed eyes searching for his features. He could feel his temples throb and his entrails stretched and rattled from the tension. Now or never, he gauged.

"Why don't you and I take a walk into the bushes?" Kirk stood, lifting the fellow up by the arm, contemplating the man's solid weight. "Come on, I know a good spot." He pushed the man ahead of him. The man hesitated. Kirk stated, "It's all right, I understan'." This seemed to ease the big fellow's doubt. Kirk followed his broad shoulders down the path.

They crossed the football field and kicked the dust in the uneven places.

"Where's the place?" asked the man doubtful. Kirk judged the man's attitude, cautious, maybe willing to back out, but so far no noise from the bushes. Just two quiet people in a quiet, lonely spot.

"Over there." Kirk pointed his finger at the bench in the shadows. The fellow stopped by the bench. When Kirk heard Big Gump moving out from the bushes, he struck with all the strength his powerful forearms could generate. The man started to whimper. Once, twice, three times the pistons moved. Sharp, ear-clattering cracks in the night. Gump was in on it now. Coolly, methodically, they worked on the sobbing lump. Their arms moving so fast and close that they were jarring each other. Kirk pointed his left and a half-loop haymaker coming from the empty night carrying with it the heartaches of three lonesome years; it was a heavy tank jarring and lifting the man over the bench. He got up to run. Leaping, Kirk overtook him after five yards. He grabbed him from behind, careful not to be thrown over the man's shoulders. His hand clamped the man's mouth, muffling a scream. Gump in front now, and the bony fist jarring the man's teeth, the blows crushing Kirk's hand into the mouth and teeth. He could feel the sticky blood in his hands, he released his hand, and with one sinking stomach blow and Gump's fist deflated the gas bag. An ear-splitting shriek sent a tracer out into the park. Big Gump directed one kick and the head jerked back like a pogo-stick.

Expertly they rifled the pockets. Breathing deeply, Kirk pulled the watch from the man's shirt. While ripping off one shoe, Kirk saw the flashlight come into the path two hundred feet away.

Into the bushes quickly. They moved down through rough underbrush coming to their known path and across a grass stretch their speed catapulting them onto the sidewalk. Gump jarred a boy walking with his girl, but not stopping they crossed the street. At Harper, Kirk moved into a passageway hearing Gump's heavy tread behind him. Out into the backyard, across and over a fence. Then running along the railroad tracks, stopping where the path entered Sixty-first Street. Now easily. Their steps slower. Kirk felt his lungbox sob, he wiped his face with a handkerchief, noticing the big gash in his palm, blood bubbling but not too fast. He wrapped the handkerchief around the palm. He led Gump to the tunnel and they entered, turning the corner up the stairs and down the dark hall. Gump had the key in the door. The room's smell was stale, tobacco-like, cabbage-like.

"Christ, your joint's crappier than mine." Kirk looked over the disarray. Gump handed him a cheap quart of whisky almost full. He felt the warmth in his throat filling his insides, expanding his person. Taking the neck of the bottle he splashed some on his palm rewrapping the handkerchief and fell to the bed.

The loot was on the bedsheet. A wallet, some cards, fifty-one dollars, change, a Bulova watch, a diamond-numbered model.

"We connected, uh, Kirk?" said Gump and to Kirk he was an evil Paris apache, swarthy, with one scar on his face; but to friends a mild, meek, easy-going bum, a good-natured roughneck.

"We'll split the dough and dump the watch later." Gump nodded. This had been understood. Kirk would handle the essentials. Gump's mind was like the ocean, slow but irrepressible, and Kirk was smiling, his arm around Gump and the bottle passed between their hands.

The music blared from the opened windows, tumbled into the newly rainfilled gutter, slid with the murky water, dropping a broken shoelace down the drain. Saturday night and the cars parked bumper to bumper along the curb. Up in the Casino the jitterbugs kicking out before the crowd came. Floor dim and blue. Blue lights intermingling with the trumpet's glissade. The sound of a sax blue and mellow.

Kirk sat at the bar watching the dancers through

the pillars, and Big Gump across from him was hard at work on a whisky and coke.

"Give," Kirk said. "What's your so secretive news?" He watched Gump's swarthy face, the powder-blue lights giving it a gunmetal sheen.

"No more jackrolling," Gump said. "The park's hotter than a firecracker. Someone knocked over a dick by mistake."

"Barney told me this afternoon. So we lay off for a few weeks until the heat's gone. Is that the big news?"

"No, Martin's back!"

Kirk's fingers gripped the table. "Where?" he demanded.

"I saw him downtown.... He lives on the Northside for his job. He said he was moving back."

"Back where?"

"Here. Sixty-third. He was worryin' about you being mad. I said you weren't."

"You take one hell of a lot for granted."

"He's gonna show here."

"Tonight!"

"Yep," Gump said.

Kirk watched Gump's fingers like oily pale serpents twisting the straw.

"I wasn't going to tell you. Martin said not to. He was going to surprise you ... Don't go off half cocked. He's gonna make things right."

Kirk gulped his drink. Only two things had preyed on his mind in prison. Jeannie and Martin. Tonight like manna from heaven, they would both be here. Both would be knocked over, only in different ways. He wouldn't rough Martin in the dance hall. No, better than that, coax him outside. He visualized Martin ass down on the sidewalk, cringing. But don't let that oily smooth bastard start talking, Kirk cautioned himself. Martin could sell parkas up the

Amazon. Edge him outside between dances and then
later sew Jeannie up in her apartment. Two birds with
one stone. And Kirk had satisfaction in the
anticipation. "Are you sure?" he asked. A smile
crossing his face, and his big hands opened and
closed.

"Sure about what?"

"That Marty will be here, stupid."

"That's what he said. He said late."

Kirk downed the drink. In the coke the whisky
mellowed down and wasn't bad. Kirk reached into his
inner pocket, to make sure he hadn't forgot the fat
letter of Jeannie's. He relit his cigar and walked
between the pillars.

The floor was crowded with the Casino
Saturday-nighters. Five days a week the bodies would
bend and struggle in the steel mills, foundries, offices
and factories with what they called work. Tonight,
under the colored lights, over the waxed rectangular
floors, between the high marble pillars, and opened
windows with the throbbing jolting music and wafts
of cheap aftershave lotion and Tabu, their bodies
meshed, jarred and struggled with what they called
pleasure. Kirk looked over the bobbing heads,
watching the shifting of feet. The rhythm soaked into
his brain, causing his temples to throb. He turned
toward the orchestra.

Jeannie was standing near the corner by the
bandstand. And it was as if a firecracker had
exploded. Even the trumpeter peered over the shiny,
yellow, oil-glistened instrument at the big, black
picture hat. The good modeling in the face depicted a
smooth panther, black and sleek. Kirk looked into the
brown eyes, deep, somber and liquid.

When he stepped to the floor, her pelvis crawled
against his. His muscular forearm grooved deep into

her waist's tender flesh. No sliver of light interrupted their dovetailed bodies, and Jeannie's yearning, mischievous movement said, the closer the bone the sweeter the meat.

Two hours later Kirk waited with Jeannie for the beginning of the eighth dance.

He followed the faces along the sideline. He could see Big Gump, cadaverous, looking glum and blurred with the rest of the faces. The murky, green-blue light made the pale blurred faces resemble fish in an aquarium bowl. Kirk readjusted his eyes to the dim, smoky light. The dancers were shadows pasted upright against the temporary silence. The music set their bodies in motion, dissolving the shadows into stringed marionettes, convulsing and jerking.

Jeannie moved slowly, easily. Her rear would swing back into the Bronze Age and every time the hips came back Kirk trembled with anticipation. The picture hat had been checked and the mass of brown hair framed her features. Her body, held in by a magician's rig, seemed ready to burst from the dress. She didn't press too much. Her head was back with her hands grasped behind his neck.

"I'm resting, Kirk. Do you mind?"

She rubbed her cheek against his. He could feel her eyelashes tickle like a centipede's feelers.

"Can you keep a secret?" She drew back and her features blurred. "Next week I'm going to Miami."

"How long?"

"Month or so."

"Work or pleasure?"

"You're getting to be a question bug."

"Only because you are so secretive."

She worked her body as if she didn't hear, increasing her movement, coming close, pasting him indelibly. Her perfume filtered into his nostrils. This was not Tabu with its garish reek. Something better, much better and in keeping with the soft glazed film of her inky dress.

"What is this?" He nuzzled her ear where the perfume was the strongest.

"Guess?"

"Tabu," he lied.

"You're joking, Kirk. It's *Moment Supreme* by Patou. You can only get it in Carson or Fields and some of the exclusive shops."

"Oh! Nuts!"

"Don't be silly, when a girl's in show business she has to wear the best."

As the music ended, Jeannie walked ahead of him to the bar. Even in her walk she was dogging it. Kirk watched the expressions on the other women's faces. Not envy, but sheer hatred.

"What will you have?"

She ordered a Stinger. He watched the bartender hold the bottle so Jeannie could see the label. Then the hair-backed hands assembled the crème de menthe laying a film over the brandy. Kirk took some bourbon, neat. One drop spilled, and the varnish curled as if touched by a soldering iron. He shifted uneasily on the high round stool, his nervous toes tapping the chrome cylindrical rungs.

"Why are you looking around?" she asked.

"Waiting for Martin. He was supposed to show here. You remember Marty?"

"Do I. He almost took me apart at Phil's party. Did you forget that night? ... How late are we going to stay tonight?" she added hastily.

"Maybe we can go downtown. Hit some spots."

"Not tonight, Kirk. I'll powder myself now, we can go home early."

Gump appeared at his side. "I watched you two on the dance." He gestured to Jeannie's disappearing figure. "That doll could put a piece of chalk in her back porch, spell Mississippi and dot all the I's."

The light in her apartment was on as they came down the street. Jeannie's pace decreased.

"Did you leave the light on?" Kirk asked. The street light was in back of them. He could see her face. She had stopped. There was a minute of silence. "Did you?"

"I must have," said Jeannie. Her teeth glittered as they approached the next street light. He could see Jeannie's lips, with the shadow they seemed big, sullen. His premonition told him he wouldn't get to them. The chance of white sheets and a squirming baby-pink body rolled past Kirk's eyes like a boxcar going past a bum on a rainy night.

"Kirk, it's been nice."

"Ain't I coming up?"

"Some other night. We have plenty of time. I'm not leaving town for a week." Her laugh was hollow.

He fought back the urge to smear her face, just once. Scatter the pearlies. Ruin the lips for little fat Mr. Otis.

She held her arms out and he hesitated. One arm went around his neck and her lips sprawled over his. A long kiss, the going-away kind.

She was up the stairs and he could see the black fluff of her dress vanish around the landing. Jeannie would fix her lips on the top floor. He imagined seeing her walk into the apartment. Mr. Otis had moved from buzzerman to keeper of the keys in one week. Whatever he had must be potent. The pearls and the black dress. Jeannie was no sucker. Kirk sat on the steps and drank the remaining half of the bottle. He was mad at his own inadequacy. He stepped to the sidewalk. Stood still, watching the apartment. He heard laughter; and saw a man's shape come to the window and pull down the shades.

Kirk looked around the street. He walked down part way where it was dark between lights. He found Mr. Otis's long chrome Lincoln.

He waited motionless for two minutes. He looked at the apartment. The light was out.

"Kirk, it's been nice."

He spat on the sidewalk. Hastily he went to the roadster and flattened the four tires. He threw the caps away. One vicious snap and the car's aerial lay in the gutter. Wrapping his handkerchief around his fist making it into a compact knot, and one quick jab carried the window glass into the car. The glass fell on the soft seats and made no noise.

At the alley, Kirk took out the letter, ripped it into little pieces. At least the letter problem was settled. This was one letter in the ashcan that Jeannie wouldn't see again. He remembered Big Gump and wondered if Martin had showed.

The dance closed at two, couples and strays heading in all directions. Big Gump was gone, leaving Kirk to stand alone under the lattice shadows of the El. He tilted the pint bottle, the liquor leaving his tongue bitter. As he walked, the gold leaf he had painted over the city, while in prison, vanished. The city's structures were silent and ominous as if some gigantic, mysterious drop-forge had left a city of corroded steel and acid. Overhead Kirk heard the rushing roar of a jet plane. His eyes dropped to look at the street. Never had he seen the streets so crummy. The city was becoming a big trash bucket with the Sixty-third neighborhood leading the pack.

His foot picked up a paper which wrapped around his leg with every step. He stopped to unwrap the paper and kick at it viciously until it dropped into the littered gutter with the rest of the night's accumulated debris. Soon the blue Hawaiians would be over Cottage Grove moving in lock, stock and baggage. "I give you Chicago," Kirk blurted out loud, his words turned inward in remorse and Kirk stopped to confront the silent street. One beautiful dungheap with gridironed miles of garbage. Chicago with its special cathedrals: the bars, stripjoints, dance halls, bookies and honky-tonks. Land of the Tasmanian Dodge where the high priests were the suave tuxedoed owners and politicians. He tilted the bottle again to drain the remaining half, and then sent it scaling, to crash and splinter against the elevated brace; until each tiny piece glinted in the smoky yellow light, and then smoldered in his heavy lidded eyes like campfires on a barren wasteland.

Martin's failure to appear, and the behavior of Jeannie, disturbed him. Where was Jeannie now? Would it be some sort of high-class strip, piece by piece, until Mr. Otis dissolved into one bead of sweat, or perhaps recline deep in a bubble bath, the foam caressing her as she built up adrenalin for Mr. Otis, impatient and grotesquely fat. Jeannie in the tub steaming over a letter, opening like a clam. Mr. Otis would be waiting restlessly, to dip deep into the deep red of the suggestive lips. Kirk wracked his head. Perhaps it was different, something past his limited imagination. He walked up the apartment steps, the dimness and musty odors clogging his pores, creeping over his body.

Kirk stopped, thinking momentarily, and then the dime was in the phone. A buzz and kickback following each number. He waited in the dimness listening to the buzz. Hopefully he redialed Jeannie's number. No answer. They're there, he realized. The buzzing might throw them off key, or Jeannie would be explaining and both would laugh. With one surge, Kirk's hand looped to smash into the phone. The knuckles pulled away bruised. People were getting up. He could hear anxious voices.

Inside the apartment, he braced his back against the door. One finger rubbed the bruised knuckles. His laugh was empty. In this corner at one hundred eighty-five pounds and almost six feet, Kirk Wagner, and in this corner one Bakelite telephone. "Jesus, are you ever tough?" Kirk said to himself. And while he gulped the whisky, the meanness and anxiety over Jeannie transferred to Martin.

Lying in bed, the sweat moist under his pajama top, Kirk worked the patterns through his mind. Martin coming up the street. Kirk easy, lurking, waiting. Hello, you four-flusher, and one left, a hard one. Martin was a sucker for a feint to the stomach and a looping hook, maybe a bolo punch ... The scenes became more violent. Always Martin minus teeth, spitting them out on the sidewalk, into the sewer overflow. Kirk stayed awake, restless in the heat and the Midway full of families spreading their blankets, the children happy under the big gas-flame sky, voice in the dark, the train whistle threading junction stop into your heart, a pulling wail, curling away from the Smokies over the Blue Grass, past Little Egypt, meet me in St. Louey.

CHAPTER III

Two weeks had passed since the dance. Jeannie, Kirk thought, would be toasting her obscene toes in the Miami Beach sand. He visualized her parading around in some half ounce of suit like a proud pedigree in heat. And nearby would be the little fat waddling poodle called Mr. Otis. And since the dance, no word about Marty. Perhaps Big Gump had been mistaken.

Kirk looked around cautiously before he entered the playground's washroom. Once inside, he set things up fast. He hung the tattered khaki short coat over the metal frame around the toilet, extracted a small bar of soap from the pocket and the ivory-handled razor blade. The Twinworks symbol on the blade was caked with the previous day's soap. Quickly, he washed his arms and lathered his face. He liked the easy scrape of the blade. He could hock the razor and might have to later. Face smooth now, he looked into the mirror. He was tan from the park's sun. His fingers worked over the cheeks, and the fingers looked longer and bigger than ever, compared to the sunken face. His weight was in the one hundred seventies, and he had not been this low since he was sixteen. "Kirk Wagner," he said to himself, "things have got to break."

Kirk pushed the door open. The wonderful little drunken landlady had his trunk with all the shirts, clothes. Not many but she had them. And there was nothing he could do until the back rent was paid. His hand shook as he rolled the last Bull Durham cigarette.

At night the park would be full of dicks, so the jackrollin' was over. He wondered about future prospects, then pulled his coat around him. It gave him an insular feeling as he walked across the football field to the sheltered area where Big Gump's Sterno gang had their hangout. It was the same spot where they had jackrolled the mark. The previous day's wind had raked the field clear, and piled the loose papers alongside the trees at the far end. Kirk could see Big Gump and the canned heaters, as they were called. They were old men for the most part. He saw them standing around the fire as he approached. Leftovers from another generation, like Doyle, they were huddled together to squeeze the alky from the Sterno cans. From a distance they resembled bare twisted trees. Kirk crowded into the fire area. Roy, the blind man, was on the other side. His eyelids were shut, but the hands quivered like a snoose addict who put snuff on his hand and let the nostrils sniff it up. Doyle was next to him holding a long bamboo fishing pole. Even in his dirty clothes he was the best dressed one here. Doyle still had the gray jersey sweater but the unraveled sleeve had worked up to his elbow on one side. His eyes were rheumy and the only sign he gave Kirk was a slight cough.

"How's tricks, Kirk?" Gump said.

"Is that Kirk?" Roy asked, and stumbled across the fire. His feet scattered the twigs and branches almost extinguishing the flame.

"Sit down, stupid," Gump ordered.

Kirk smelled the odor of Roy, almost like sour milk. He could feel Roy's grip on his arm.

"You feel thinner, Kirk," Roy said. "Better start eating."

"I will when my ship comes in."

"You can eat tomorrow," Roy said.

Kirk recalled that Roy always had the ice-cream wagon at Harper and Sixtieth. Not much money, but enough for Roy's meager desires, beer and an

occasional bottle of hooch. After a few days' work
Roy would accumulate enough for a binge. When he
was broke, he dropped from whisky to Sterno and
then the next day would find him on the corner with
the white wagon. Kirk looked at the tousled hair and
a face the color of peanut butter. The eyes were slits
shutting out the world of light. Kirk turned to see
Doyle's shambling walk, the long bamboo pole
bobbing at his side. Doyle would try the lagoon for
pike or catfish. He never drank, Kirk remembered. A
man without vices was rare around Sixty-third, Kirk
said to himself.

"You can get fat on broken ice-cream bars
tomorrow," Roy hinted, disrupting Kirk's reverie.

Kirk looked around. Today must be rough, they
didn't have any Sterno left. He could smell the odor
of it. Their ration for the day was under the belt, and
when the sun went down they would disappear into
the doorways, alleys and junk heaps. The man next to
Kirk had rags around his feet, held tight by a thick
rubber band that was cut from an old inner tube. This
crew was in the same fix as the New Orleans paupers
and when the final day came they would get no
trombone-trumpet departure. Kirk thought of Tulane
University with the fancy southern belles shaking
their compact prats around the campus. Shades of old
Aunt Hager's Blues. His mind alerted when another
Sterno came smashing through the brush. He spoke
rapidly into Big Gump's ear. Kirk strained to hear.
Big Gump jumped up.

"Kirk, are you in? There's a case of alky in a truck
off Sixty-third. The driver's in at the cafe."

Kirk noticed Gump's slow gesture. Gump was
barreled. He didn't look it while he was sitting down;
but now when he was standing, his figure wavered
like the rest. Roy was crowding them, his ears almost

moving forward.

"What alky?" Roy asked.

"I'm out, Gump." Kirk moved away from the fire. He looked back from the pathway leading out of the park. Gump, Roy and six others were in a huddle, arms around one another. Kirk pulled his feet along the path. He didn't want the pokey for a bottle of alky. He was a one-time loser and besides the stuff wasn't fit to drink. For the last week his mouth had watered over hot coffee and the steaming trays he had seen people carry in the cafeteria. He was wise to the effect of alky on a stomach unlined by food. A quick trip to the marble orchard. He couldn't take it like the Sternos whose stomachs were inured to anything, and whose metabolism craved alky before food. He walked across the street, down Sixtieth, toward the small stores past the viaduct. He tried all the bakeries along the carline and ended at Woodlawn with two fresh rolls and a stale loaf of bread.

Air hammers burped, and the work gang between the two ponies was surrounded by chalky dust. Up on Sixty-third another crew was slopping red paint on the elevated stanchions. These workmen bothered Kirk, giving him a sense of guilt at his own inactivity. There were jobs, it was just a matter of routine. He brushed the thought from his mind as his stomach gnawed, and his feet hurried toward Stony.

Barney, the cynical jockey-sized newsboy, had his hand deep in the newsie change apron. He resembled a mischievous elf, and one raised eyebrow almost joined the red curly hair. Kirk watched him hawk the papers.

"Can you spare some change?" Kirk asked.

Barney kicked his heels against the metal stand under the steps coming from the elevated. His legs looked ridiculously short as if some creator had taken a fuller lengthened body and stuck it on miniature legs. Kirk heard the change jiggling in the apron. Barney's hand came out with a quarter and a dime.

"Not that much."

"Take it, or I'll get mad."

Kirk jammed the change into the khaki coat pocket. He couldn't take any chance on holes.

"Kirk!"

"Yes," he was confronted again by the eyebrows that almost reached the hairline.

"Martin's back. Jus' saw him. He headed that way." Kirk followed the finger like a pointer, and it seemed that ice tongs had pierced through his ribs to meet point to point somewhere in his heart.

Kirk saw him when he entered Metzner's bookie. Martin, big as day and twice as gaudy in a flowery red shirt, covered with a neat gray sharkskin. A Panama was cocked over the delicate, evenly featured face, and a slender panatella stuck in his white teeth. Martin hadn't changed, only the eyes had dissipated circles. Kirk's heart skipped a beat, and when Martin reached for the cigar the canary-yellow two-carat ring hit him like the Lindbergh Beacon.

"Marty, is it you?" Kirk's fingers trembled and the knees went watery. In the moment of indecision, with his stomach gnawing, he had the feeling like watching one's horse in a stretch drive, trembling and nervous. His mouth dry as cotton, he hesitated.

Martin's face was calm but not a trace of a smile. Calm but expectant. Kirk's mind flashed back to prison. The long, cold nights came back with a surge. He watched Martin's jaw muscle begin to twitch.

Martin's voice was almost an inaudible whisper. "I've come back to make things right."

Kirk realized Martin's mood was one he had never

seen. Martin was weighing his chances. The cockiness subdued. Subdued behind the realization that his acceptance depended on Kirk. The neighborhood would always back the man who took the rap, and kept his mouth shut. Martin was in a spot. But Kirk understood his own weakness. Martin was in the chips, he must be. The hovering shadow of ending up with the Sterno gang pushed Kirk into a bad corner. Kirk had no course but to hear him out. He followed the extended hand.

He knew he had deliberated too long. The previous week's anger had disappeared and the entire mood was one of envy. In the short interval Kirk hardly remembered shaking Martin's hand and the dream of retaliation had almost vanished.

Doyle had entered the bookie's front and moved over to the side contrasting Martin's sensitive alert features.

"Finally hit, Marty," Kirk said, and even Doyle's face was one of amazement. The prodigal had returned.

"Where'd you hit the loot?" asked Izzy the counterman.

"Hollywood," said Martin. "There's gold dust on every street and all that's necessary is brains. Like I always said, a nice-looking young man like me will go far. Right, Kirk?" By now Hutch had gathered with Doyle and Izzy, and in a big way Kirk felt proud.

"What's the joint like?" asked Hutch, who resembled King Farouk.

"Hollywood's like a South Chicago whorehouse, the madams drunk, the girls are getting it and nobody's hitting the till," answered Martin exhaling the words around the smoke.

"Why did you come back to the neighborhood?" asked Izzy.

"Sixty-third Street isn't a neighborhood. It's a disease," answered Martin. Kirk recalled Jake's duplicate words.

"Don't interrupt," Hutch said to Izzy. "What about the place?"

"How would you like to take a star out on the beach, and all she's got on is a sable coat and high heels?" Martin named a well-known movie starlet and Doyle's eyes shifted.

Hutch said, "Well, I'll be a son-of-a-bitch."

"Champagne." Martin hooked one finger in his belt, filled the room with cigar smoke, looked at Kirk. "And drank it out of her slipper. Careful to plug the toe of course."

"Of course," said Hutch.

"Then we had lobster in one of the Santa Monica joints. Mind you she's walking around in those champagne-soaked slippers, with nothing on underneath and every time she moves the customers can see Broadway."

"It's unbelievable, but a guy could waste his time in Chi without ever knowing how to live.... And then you could have knocked me over with a feather, when up in her apartment she shows me she has a glass right eye."

Martin extracted a big long cigar. He handed it to Kirk. Kirk read the label: Partagas. The cigar was over half a foot long. He smelled the aroma, fingered the soft tobacco. He toyed with the cigar almost afraid to light it.

"What happened about the eye?" said Hutch.

"You know how those movie broads are," said Martin. "Perverted, that's the word; isn't it, Doyle?"

Kirk watched Doyle's face redden.

"Go on," said Hutch.

"She never did put the thing back in. It all

happened on the couch. I heard about broads like her
…"

Kirk shook his head, his face turning into a smile.
The cigar was lit and the thick smoke tickled his
nostrils. Martin was a bunk-artist from the word go,
he thought.

"I'll be a son-of-a-bitch," said Hutch. And the
spellbinder let them have it both barrels.

"Later that night, when we went out," Martin
continued. "This tops the whole hullabaloo, she
drops her false eye in my St. Émilon."

"What's a St. Émilon?" asked Doyle.

"See that," Martin hit Kirk's arm. "Your boy is
gone for a couple years and he is able to stump
Doyle." He blew some cigar smoke around Doyle's
neck. "St. Émilon is a French drink that makes people
do things they want to do and can't." And when
Martin nodded, all gathered around him nodded
understandingly.

Martin gathered his flock, escorted them out the
door. He pointed his arm toward a low, pale-green,
new Cadillac.

"What is that?" Kirk asked.

"That's the red wagon I didn't have when I was a
kid," Martin said.

"Caligula's horse deified in chrome," said Doyle.

"A little gift from my honey, for taking care of
her. If you know what I mean," said Martin.

And Hutch said, "I know what you mean."

Kirk pulled in his breath.

Doyle said, "They sow not; yet they reap."

The Cadillac weaved like a drunken boxer around
the Jackson Park curves, and Kirk could feel the
warm summer breeze filtering into his senses. By now,
Martin had bloated him with Hollywood stories

involving a president of the First National Bank, and all he could do was believe when Martin had flashed a wallet full of bills.

The Cadillac was heading downtown where they would eat. And on the way down Martin kept talking.

"And the four of us were going from the racetrack, down to Ensenada ... me, the drunken astrologer, the Mexican general, and the redheaded Hungarian Jewess. Just like I mentioned before, the sailfish ate the astrologer, and the last I saw of the General and the Hungarian they were driving off in a Standard Oil truck."

Kirk knew Martin was reaching for them.

"What did you do in that predicament?"

"No predicament. I sent a letter to my honey. And hocus-pocus the telegram with dough is there. Remind me to tell you about the race horse I owned that would only eat orchids."

"Cut the crap, Martin. You and I can kid the others but let's not kid each other. Is any of that fancy stuff true?"

"None of it. None ... Oh, yes. I was out in Hollywood but all I ever did there was tip over a Chinese crapper on Halloween."

"Keep it up, brother, and I'll be remembering about that money and the three years up the river."

"Forget it. I'm buying you a suit today, and you won't have to be stemming those bastards or laying around with floosies."

"So you know everything?"

"Yes, I know everything," Martin said.

And Kirk guessed that he did.

Martin's room in the Shoreline Hotel was plain, chaste, and the fish-laden smell came in from the lake, rippling the curtains. Kirk was pleasantly full. A thick, New York-cut steak under his belt and the strong Cuban aroma of the cigar Martin had bought him made his head giddy. It was an Upmann. He had never known cigars like this existed for little people. This smoke was for the stock exchanges, and people who rode the big ships for France; but apparently in this airtight system of the chosen few there was a loophole and Martin—no doubt about it now—had found it.

Where would Martin get the money to purchase the heavy Brazilian alligator shoes and the smooth tan fifty-dollar gabardine for him? And by then he would not have been amazed if Martin had bought him a Malacca cane. When he had seen the cash purchase receipt for the Cadillac made out in Martin's name, it had cast all doubts aside. Martin had found the loophole.

"Sit over here, Kirk." He motioned to the bed. Tossing his Panama on the dresser, Martin bent low and pulled a suitcase from under the bed. It was on the bed opened, and Kirk followed Martin's hands as he went under the shirts and extracted three stacks of bills. Tens, new shiny tens. Passports to Nirvana. Martin pulled off the band and fanned the tens. A hundred to the stack as Kirk knew.

"This is no California bankroll. Two tens around a lemon."

"Marty, you hit gold." And Kirk could say no more.

Marty restacked the bills. They went under the shirts. The suitcase back under the bed and Kirk with his forehead furrowed said to himself, this was too much, much too much. "Where did you strike?"

"I'll let you in on the whole scoop. The entire story, but not now," He pushed Kirk toward the shower. "Shower down. We have things to do. I'll give you the entire story tomorrow and Kirk, you're in."

Kirk applied the lather. And with the first spray of warm water tingling against his skin a wave of optimism built up Kirk's limbs and goose pimples formed on his skin.

It was ten o'clock when they arrived at the Club Rabelais on Rush Street. A leftover blind-pig from prohibition days, it was downstairs in a brownstone. Kirk strode by the grated fence and followed Martin down the foot-polished steps. The new suit tickled his skin, and Martin's twenty-dollar bill in his pocket had helped restore his ego. Once inside, the place was larger than he had expected. A bar ran along one side, and there was a small pedestal for a bandstand with a tiny floor sandwiched between the circular tables. One wall was painted with amorphous shapes, the only figures Kirk could discern were a chemist's vial and a guitar.

The far wall had original oil paintings, and small white cards numbered in black gave the artist's price. Beards, people who looked like Zouaves, flowing-gowned Hindus, all very noisy and tangy in the layers of blue smoke that hung four feet over the patrons' heads. Kirk knew the type of place. Half a mixture between the gay underworld and college crowd, the Club Rabelais was currently fashionable. In a few years it would be old hat, and one would have to go elsewhere to hear cool bop or whatever was the rage. The international, gay school-girly flavor would be gone, only to return again to the Rabelais years later when it was again first on the popularity circuit. People would refer to it as *The* place one year out of five. It had been popular in the year that people could walk across the Hudson on the

top of silk hats, and would still be in circulation when
ordinary citizens wore wrist-watch radios and made
trips to the moon. The Club Rabelais furnished an
outlet to the people who shoved against the current
trend. A place to find bedroom partners of originality.
Kirk wondered how Martin had stumbled on the
place.

"There they are," said Martin and Kirk followed
him through a colorful underbrush of people.

Deep in the corner at one of the circular tables
with a multicolored candle stuck in a gooseneck
bottle, Martin stopped.

"Honey, you're late." The girl wore a blue beret.
Her bangs cut crisp, lay across her forehead, and the
Harlequin glasses gave an intellectual sophisticated
look.

"This is Marie," Martin said and she pulled
Martin to the seat, with Martin still gesturing. "And
Kirk this is Lisette. Lisette ... Kirk."

The girl had risen, and Kirk appraised a pale
blonde built like a reed, with silken hair like spun
fiber drawn into a tight Ubangi bun placed directly on
top of her head. The blue denim skirt and blue silk
blouse set off the face smooth as glass. Martin had
chosen their dates well. Kirk looked around at the
yummy yoghurt crowd and was surprised by the
countless bearded young men. There were more
beards in the Rabelais than he had seen in ten years.
He turned to concentrate on Lisette.

The placid faces of three Negroes muddled into
amorphous wall figures. Their music erratic and
discordant. Kirk rose from the cocktail glass on the
table, chilled tall and sedate and followed Lisette to
the floor.

Mashed together, the noise trickled into Kirk's
head and rattled like tumblers in a steel cup. He

remembered Martin's words in the washroom, Lisette will play, only she wants to hear the dice bounce off the backboard. He pulled her close, their bodies remaining in one spot due to the overloaded floor and Lisette's sponge shoes.

"Am I holding you too close?" Kirk asked.

"Make it easy on yourself."

"How did Martin find this place?" Kirk asked.

"He didn't. We found it."

"And Martin found you?"

"Not exactly.... Marie was walking around the paddock at Washington Park and ran into your friend. He does own horses, doesn't he?"

"I guess he *does*."

"What do you mean by that?"

"Martin owns so many things. Sometimes it is hard to keep track."

"Marie was infatuated by him.... I was often sorry, I hadn't walked around the paddock instead."

"Meaning I'm no bargain."

"Don't be so self-analytic."

When they danced near the table, Kirk could see Marie laughing. Martin the horseman, Martin the stimulating conversationalist. She was infatuated with him now. Martin would be with her one week, maybe two. Hot and cold. Charm to sudden larceny. The only certain thing about Marty was his ability to take care of Number One.

The music had ended.

"How do you like Chicago now?" Martin asked as Kirk seated Lisette.

"Very primitive. Your friend is a good dancer," said Lisette. Kirk's face glowed from the expensive sherry. It escaped his imagination to remember shaving in the park's washroom, then Gump's Sterno gang, and now to be here in a striking position with

Martin back, financially loaded, and the two lush girls as dates.

"Primitive. Do you hear that, Kirk?" asked Martin. "Ask Lis', she knows class. The kid just came back from Europe." Martin was getting looped. Kirk could tell. Within five drinks, the girl had progressed from Lisette to Lis', and now to the kid.

"Where were you?" asked Kirk.

"Paris, Switzerland, the Riviera," answered Lisette. Marie interrupted: "Lisette, why don't we take the boys up to your place."

"In one second." She rose to walk to the washroom.

Kirk toyed with the glass, how anyone could sit or dance to this discordant blare was beyond him. He strained to listen to Marie, snuggly, her arms entwined around Martin.

"You promised you would have some," the almost inaudible whisper toyed with Martin's ear. "Lisette is only in for a few days. Her folks are gone for the week-end. I told her..."

"We can pick some up. I know a place." Martin was grinning.

They all rose when Lisette appeared. Following the two girls through the crowd, Martin jeered

"Kirk, you're so primitive."

"I'll primitive her Vassar fanny for her." And he followed Martin out the door.

Martin pulled to a stop near a small pool hall on Broadway. Marie dialed the radio, Kirk sat patiently waiting. Lisette was at the far end of the seat, her red, fingernailed hands lay alongside like a barrier. She had made no attempt to be snuggly like Marie. Kirk watched Martin hurrying back. As he passed the street light, he looked like a movie version of a lawyer or an F.B.I. man, neat, not a hair out of place, the good-looking, symmetrical, Irish face grinning. The ring sparkled from the street light like an incandescent flame. He patted his pocket as he slid under the steering wheel.

"You darling," Marie said pressing close as the Cadillac purred.

Kirk attempted to pull Lisette closer.

"Not now," she said coolly.

The Cadillac was passing the Gold Coast. The building tops perforating the blue-black sky.

The apartment was along the Gold Coast. Lisette drew back the drapes, and the Lake front panorama showed blinking lights in a blue-black sky. Kirk took in the heavy drapes, the tapestry above the walnut bookcase. He moved sensitively between the cushions piled in the room's center, to glance at the rack of record albums next to the teakwood Capehart: Leadbelly, Bartok, Hindemith. Christ, does Martin know what he is doing? Kirk was baffled. These weren't his type of people. Martin's small wad couldn't pay a month's rent for this place. Lisette had been cool to him. Why had she even bothered to have a date? There must be a common denominator.

"What a chateau," Martin said, sinking himself comfortably deep in the couch, a long deep Charles of London. The pointed polished shoes rested on a five hundred dollar piece of marble. On the low marble coffee table was a bottle of Harvey's Bristol Dry Sherry, and four narrow fluted glasses.

Martin had the cigarette case out. Cigarettes were rough-cut as if handmade.

"Goodies," Lisette said, placing the narrow-fluted glass gently to the marble.

"Careful," Martin said. "These are not cut. They'll blow your wig."

"Daddy, why are you so good to me?" Marie said,

her knees on the couch, her arms hugging him.

"In a minute," Martin said. "Kirk, try one. Just for kicks. You're too nervous, boy. Much too nervous."

Lisette had propped herself on the cushion, and soon her eyes had the listless dullness, the pupils enlarging.

Kirk puffed viciously on the cigarette and a wave of utter relaxation came over him. In the wavy room Marie had placed some records on the machine, and Martin was dancing with her, and soon the music lingered, but Martin and bang hair were gone.

"Ladybug, ladybug, fly away home. Your house is on fire, and your children alone." The sponge shoes were in the corner. Lisette hummed and purred, flitting across the room in a mock ballet pantomime. Leaping from the table to chairs and over the spongy cushions, flicking the slender ivory legs, showing flashes of white filmy panties popularized by a tennis star. One more gallop around, around the room and her body flew to the couch beside Kirk. "Sugar, I'm higher than a witch's wig." Her breath came in short gasps.

Kirk sunk lower overcome by drowsiness. The effect wasn't right.

Lisette was back with two cigarettes.

"I crawled into the bedroom. Try one. Get it all in." Lisette cupped her hands, her face shifting in his vision to become clearly delineated, as he followed her instructions.

"Jeannie?"

"No, Lisette. My name's Lisette, silly. Do it like this." Her lips nibbled at the reefer end. Her mouth gasped, the lips forming a suction, a sphere shape, like a goldfish who nibbled flakes on the water. "Kirky dear."

He had slumped to the floor and she fell back beside him.

Kirk drew deep and felt the music gallop and surge in his veins like a shoot of urgent green rising from the park's earth. And then a trickle of ice water traveling with the blood stream touching his heart sporadically.

Her lips wobbled in front of his face like a crimson smoke ring, all askew, against the glassy, icy, syringe frostness of her face.

"Are you smoky inside? Come into Lisette's room," she tickled his chin.

"Go away." Kirk pushed the grinning face from him.

He was standing, brushing imaginary specks from his pants. His feet moved high over the cushions that had grown immeasurably larger. Kirk reached for the cigarette butt on the black and white marble.

Lisette had curled on the couch. She was smiling.

"You don't like me." She stretched luxurious and slow, with her hands high over her head.

Kirk moved cautiously. He must not stumble. The walls before him chalky-white, unscarred by any tapering finger. From the square-windowed bars to the Gold Coast penthouse. Success in one easy lesson, in one easy month. Thanks to Marty's jewel-studded wallet. He stopped to combat the darkness, his big fingers clutching and grasping. He was trying hard to stand.

"Don't go way, sugar."

She was up coaxing, coyly, vivaciously, the arms white and snaky clean. "Follow me. Oh my, my legs feel like French rococo chair legs."

The bedroom was orange, a soft satiny orange, the oversize bed in one corner flanked by reflective wall mirrors and one mirror overhead.

Her face came closer nibbling at his throat and ears.

"You missed too many boats from Paris, kid," Kirk murmured.

Kirk whispered to the girl. She was beautiful, long dark hair like Jeannie's. He could see his fingers reach out for her, they were distorted and long as if he were seeing them in an inverted beer stein. He wiggled the elongated fingers.

When he awoke there was only Lisette. She was in a ripped slip. One eye was black and blue and swollen. Her hairdo was down. He looked around. On the dresser were the empty bottles. He swung his feet to the floor. It was full of ashes, marijuana butts and spilled whisky. His eyes focused back to Lisette, her face was horrible. She looked wild as she approached him—

"Get up, you hoodlum," she said.

"I said I'm sorry." He went to touch her shoulder, Lisette jerked away—

"After what you did last night! Just get out, you bum. That's what you can do."

Kirk's fingers found a pack of crumpled cigarettes. There was one inside, it was ripped in the middle and the twisted strands showed. He broke it in half, stuck one piece in his mouth. His mind tried to bring itself up to time.

"What happened to the wall?"

"You! You!" she screamed. "Running down the hall without clothes and scribbling with my lipstick on the walls. And hitting me twice." She held her head.

Kirk wanted to say something. What, he did not know. He looked from the dresser to Lisette, then to the wall. Where were Martin and Marie? He wondered.

"How 'bout?" He pointed to the door to the other bedroom.

"They're gone. Yesterday. Look at me."

"I'm sorry."

"Sorry, after acting like a crazy man."

He heard her rambling, but his mind pictured his own body jumping up and down like a circus bear. He looked at his hand. One finger was cut.

Lisette was crying, her shoulders jerked up and down in spasm. Kirk searched for his clothes. The only shirt there was Martin's and when he put it on, he had to laugh. He looked like a boob. The cuffs came to his elbows. He imagined Martin wandering around with sleeves dragging to his knees.

"Go ahead, laugh, you hoodlum."

"I said I'm sorry." He went to touch her shoulder. Lisette jerked away.

"Just get out. That's what you can do."

When he came out on the street, his feet wobbled as an ice-skater does after taking off his skates. A sharp pain shot through his ankle. The day was fading; lights were coming on.

"What day is this?" he said to a lantern-jawed doorman standing under a canopy.

"Tuesday, boy, and you are lost."

"You can say that again," Kirk said. His legs became steadier as he moved toward the curb. "Shoreline Hotel," he directed the cabbie.

CHAPTER IV

Kirk walked into the cigar store with Martin. This was no dummy run. Funny that he would be shaking inside like Big Gump when he was on the nose candy. Kirk's hands were slick with sweat, and the blood sent a warm surge through his face. He stood transfixed, half in the store, half outside. The street was clear; the morning pleasant with high clouds rib-patterned and racing along, nature's horses jockeyless, odds no rain, and the track fast.

He could see and hear Martin. Vague voices in a slipshod reverie. What a bull artist, Martin. They were outside in the street, the clouds gone and the plate-glass sky still overhead.

"Did you follow the jive?" asked Martin, leading toward the car.

"Just as you said, Marty. No slip-ups." Kirk seated himself in the black two-door Ford.

"Have a smoke." Martin's extended hand held a pack of Camels. "The next place I get gum, then cigars, then pipe tobacco. After that some candy. Then more cigs, different brand. Before you know it, the day's over."

"Always work in the mornings?" asked Kirk.

"Naw break it up. Set up a pattern the bulls can't figure. Except in this game it's the Treasury Department." Martin stopped for a light. "You can see, Kirk. Always have a good bill ready. Case your situation if you have to leave fast. I'll explain more as we go along."

"What kind of rap goes with this?"

"No rap. We play it smart, pass a bundle and leave town. Then you do what you want to do. Just watch me."

And Martin made store after store, sometimes

talkative sometimes silent depending upon the location, mood or tone of the neighborhood. Kirk could see the Cadillac materialize out of the easy loose money. The sun was directly overhead, an orange billiard ball with the number burned off, and they were back in the apartment. Their new place on Sixty-fourth Street, sandwiched between a golf store and the fly-speckled lunch counter.

While Martin was in the shower and changing into less conservative clothes, Kirk held the two bills in the light. One good, one bad. Alexander Hamilton haughty and reserved on both. At the first glance Kirk couldn't notice the difference, and he sure couldn't if he didn't have both side by side. Most of Martin's conversation had soaked in. He mentally recalculated.

Take the phony money. Put it in with old coffee grounds, wear away the newness. Let them stay overnight, then a little hand wear and the bill would be as good as Uncle Sammy's. Martin was ingenious; he had all the angles worked out. Keep away from the chain stores. Hit shops with one attendant or owner. The older the person the better. Best if they were foreigners or old women. And never pass up a place where they wore glasses. Use a rented car, always a rented one, Fords if possible, good pickup car, easy maneuverability. Splatter up the plates, at least louse up a couple of numbers. One street to run for a day. Park the car. Hit two places. Always have a good bill handy. Avoid arguments, beefs, like the plague. Never use a street where they know you. Never pass a bad bill when you know someone in the joint. Carry the spare bills in the high front pocket. If caught in the act or chased head down an alley, throw the bills out after a quick turn into the alley. Come back later to get the bills, nothing wasted. Very smart, these Chinese.

One buck for every bill passed. Maybe Martin's cut was more, but he would be working for Marty. Martin was the go-between. He picked up the bills and as he had said, "He was close to the plant." Nothing to worry about for Kirk. Martin had the danger. The Treasury men always clamped at the pickup. They had no need for the *passers*.

To Kirk this all sounded too good to be true. But here was Martin passing for six months. Owned the Cadillac, good clothes, good living. Where would the escalator end?

Kirk allowed his mind free play. This wasn't even a matter of alternatives. He could be stemming beers, or food every other day, no smokes, spend half the day talking to Barney the newsboy, a frustrated Joe Humphries, or some of those Madison Street strippers sandwiched in between clean sheets. He could smell the luxuriant smoke of the Upmann in his memory, and feel the clean white red-nippled breasts run through his fingers. He could feel the quick touch of the Cadillac. What was it Marty said? He'd make me a sybarite. Kirk caught the drift; but he understood alpaca coats, cocoa-brown flannels, Miami, New York. He understood all these things and his mind was decided. The decision was easy.

"Day-dreaming, goofy?" asked Martin slipping into soft gray flannel slacks.

"An' you're sure there's no slip-ups?"

"Nothing's sure, Kirk. You know that. For the time being stick with me."

They left the apartment with plenty of time for the first race.

The first store for Kirk's valiant effort was what Martin called a pushover. A grocery place run by old folks.

Kirk pushed open the screen door and entered the world of long-hung salamis, sharp-odored cheeses. One customer ahead of him. Kirk tapped his foot nervously, stopped when he became conscious of the movement. He waited, hands behind his back, his fingers interlocked. When the woman left, Kirk walked to the counter. He placed a loaf of bread on the clean wood. The woman's eyes were watery behind the thick glasses. Her ancient face was a parrot peering back at him, mimicking his expressions. Kirk pointed to the cheese. Blocks and round loaves of cheeses, and the sandwich meats piled under the glass.

"Give me a dime's worth." His finger fell on the mincemeat.

"Which one?" He could see her head bent low, her eyes peering back at him.

"That. There." His finger was specific, anxious to be on its way, taking Kirk with it out in the clear air of the safe street.

The woman was wrapping the small bundle of meat. The string ends dangling.

Kirk fished into his pocket. Placed the ten face down on the counter. Moments later he was outside, the bills—one five, four ones and a dollar, minus sixteen cents—in change in his pocket. He moved down the street for the hardware store. Putty it was to be. A young man, getting Dad some putty for a loose window. Nothing wrong with that.

Six bills later, the Ford was entering the garage ramp. No need for the rental in the afternoon. Martin was beside him as they left the ramp on foot turning into the busy street.

"I need a drink."

Martin placed his arm around him. "You deserve one. Now wasn't it easy? Like taking candy away from a baby." A workman passed them swinging a lunch bucket. Martin tipped his hat to him and under his breath he said to Kirk, "Hello, sucker." Inside the cool bar on Halsted, rubbing elbows with the usual driftwood Kirk felt better, cooler.

"Tomorrow, kid, we step up the tempo. If you want that stake," Martin said.

Kirk nodded, sipping the cold draft beer. He was catching the drift and tomorrow he would move up the tempo.

Kirk's coffee lay on the wooden counter and his stirring made golden flecks. Outside the traffic was normal. He watched the white outfit of the girl as she moved behind the counter. Checking the clock he decided that this would be the last *pass* for the day. He had time to spare tonight. Perhaps a celebration to end the first full week as a *passer*, a full-fledged passer. Kirk mentally estimated. Four hundred ten times in six days he had risked a Federal rap. Four hundred ten times, a phony Alexander had *passed* over the counter. For each bill passed, one good dollar went into his own pocket. The rest went to Martin and moved into the symbiotic levels of a passing line to end at the *plant*. Kirk didn't know how much went to Martin; but it was a cinch that Marty wasn't getting grayer.

The metal urn glistened with oil and reflected in the concentric coffee circles on the counter. The harelipped, broad-hipped waitress stopped before him.

"Another coffee?" she asked.

Kirk returned her stare. He could sense the girl evaluating him.

"Do I pass inspection?" he asked and was immediately sorry the words slipped out.

"Pardon me," the girl said and moved quickly to refill the cup. Her arms were chubby, matching the entire shape. Kirk saw that with the taffy hair, the girl viewed from the back wasn't bad. All except for the harelip. "Is this all?" she asked.

"Yes."

Kirk watched as she bent to tally his sheet. This would be a dead cinch. He knew a come-on when he saw one. Her come-hither look was too obvious. Watching. Watching the twisted scar of the puckered lips, immediately caused the oval fullness of Jeannie's lips to come back to haunt him.

The place was empty but for them.

"Are you going?" the girl said half hesitatingly waiting for him to suggest something. Kirk wanted no part of her harelip. He felt some sympathy for her predicament, but not enough to keep from pushing the phony ten onto the counter.

He watched her fingers dance over the cash register. The change was on the counter.

"Do you have many singles?" Maybe he could force two. The girl was alone, nothing she could do but yell and he would be long gone.

"Why?"

"Could you break this also? A five and the rest in singles."

She ran her fingers in a sheaf of bills in the opened drawer.

"I think I can." The *can* sounded like *tan*. Kirk hesitated. "Drop in again," she said.

"What time does the place close?" As he talked he arranged the good money orderly into his wallet.

"We stay open all night but I get off at six." The harelip again, with the *six* sounding like *thix*. She was out on a limb dangling her quitting time before his eyes.

"I'll be back at five-thirty," Kirk said, but once his anxious feet were outside, he pushed the harelipped waitress from his mind. There was no sentimentality in this business he decided, as he turned the corner for the Ford.

The Ford was returned to the agency; and Kirk rounded the corner at Sixty-third and Stony to stop at the edge of a group of people. Roy, the blind man, was on a box lowering a mouse to his throat. A catgut string kept the live mouse's snout from opening. Roy stopped in mid-air, brought the mouse down to his side.

"I knew the bastard wouldn't do it," someone said.

"Is that goddam Hindu gonna eat the mouse?" someone else asked.

Kirk watched, Roy's lips twitched. Flecks of old roll-your-own tobacco on the lips gave it a freckled appearance like his face. What was Roy doing on the orange crate with a live mouse in his hand, Kirk wondered.

"Hit the hat, gents, and Roy ..." Big Gump jerked his thumb back to the twitching Roy. "Hit the hat and Roy will bite off its head." More people had gathered.

Gump moved in between the spectators, Kirk reached out to grab his arm. "What the hell goes?" Kirk asked.

"Dough," said Gump. "Hit the hat." Gump tried to wrench away.

"Wait a minute," Kirk said.

"What's a matter, big shot. You and Martin the only ones who can have a racket?"

"Can it, Gump, or I'll get mad." Kirk's hands tightened. He measured Gump, his eye near the Adam's apple. "Roy isn't going to bite that thing,"

Kirk's voice shook, he tried to check the tremor.

"Who said so?" Gump threatened.

"Beat it," Kirk pushed the crowd, and jumped quickly to upset the orange crate, to send Roy sprawling on the sidewalk. The small gray furry form of the mouse disappeared into a doorway to emerge and send a shadow for the gutter. Gump braced Kirk against the wall, the strong steel grip of his fingers twisting around Kirk's throat. Now or never, Kirk drove the flat of his hand across the throat and with a quick heave pushed Gump. Gump leaped forward and Kirk met his face with a leaping hook to stop Gump. Now Roy was in between struggling, screaming, "Wait, wait."

Someone yelled, "The cops."

"Here, Roy," Kirk grabbed Roy and into the tavern back to the door next to the washroom. They hurried into the dark passageway. Kirk heard footsteps behind them. He stopped, checking Ray. "Who is it?"

"It's Gump," Roy said. "I can tell his step."

"Yeh, it's me. We have somethin' to settle, Kirk."

"No more, Gump. Not friend against friend," Roy said.

Gump was near. "What's the idea. You and your angles." He pumped his hand against Kirk's sport coat. "You're eating. Afraid we might."

"Gump, you got it wrong. Only Roy doesn't need mice. Forget it and I'll stake you two. No I'll give you...."

"Kirk's meaning well," Roy said.

They walked down the passageway to enter the Wooden Shoe Club.

"Give them a drink," Kirk ordered.

"Not unless you drink with us," Roy said.

"Make it three whiskies ... Bushmill's."

"Yeh Bushmill's," said Gump. "Only the best for Kirk's friends."

Kirk couldn't detect if there was sarcasm in Gump's voice.

"Jesus, this is not like Sterno," said Roy.

"Have another," Kirk said.

"Shake with Gump, Kirk, let bygones be bygones," Roy said. "The mouse was only part his idea."

"Why didn't he bite the head off?"

"Wait a minute, big shot."

Gump was off the chair, but Roy inserted himself in-between.

"No more trouble," Roy said. "Kirk.... We didn't have any chow or liquor for two days. You were on the skids, and we ain't all lucky to have an out."

"And don't say go to work," Gump scowled.

"I'm not saying nothing. Have another drink and here." Kirk pushed a small wad of bills in Roy's hand. "Give Gump half."

While the fifth whisky went down his hatch, Kirk saw Gump hand the wad back to Roy. "There's eighteen bucks in it," Gump said. His hand came out to grip Kirk's. "Why didn't you say this in the crowd. We would have broke the deal.... Why don't you talk to Martin. I'm available."

Kirk brought his head close to Gump's and Roy's. "I will, but not yet. Not until I'm in deeper.... By the way, did you see Martin today?"

"Yeh," said Big Gump. "He went into the barbershop. They have a big game on. We tapped that bastard but didn't get a cent."

"Kirk's not one way like Marty," Roy asserted.

"Another Bushmill's, bartender," Kirk said. Inwardly the whisky had worked into his veins. He felt better, much better, and a celebration was in order. His tussle with Gump was forgotten and he leaned forward his arms around Gump and Roy. "Give us three of your best cigars, bartender."

Cards moved across the table, Martin's coat was on a hook, his chair leaned back. The red suspenders, broad and bright, added color to the white linen shirt. He's good for the night, thought Kirk, anxious to fulfill his afternoon's desire.

"How long you going to stay?" He tapped Marty's shoulder, getting dirty looks from the other players. "I'll kiss your butt in Wieboldt's window if you leave before midnight."

Martin wasn't listening but throwing in some chips after fanning the cards slightly.

"Bet two," he said.

"Can I take the keys?" Kirk's lips were close to Martin's ear.

"In the coat. Don't get blind, kid." Martin's voice followed him through the barber shop, and the attendant opened it. The air was humid from the heavy Chicago lake weather.

The Cadillac was on the outer drive, Kirk giving it spurts of gas to pass two girls in an open convertible, and he waved at them. They ignored the salutation, swerving for the long roll at Fifty-first Street. Kirk was on his way to the Wilshore, an open-air dance hall on the North Side, but he would short-circuit into the Loop for a quick one.

Kirk's first choice, the side bar of the Black Hawk, was full. He picked a small one down the street at Wabash. An older man made a place for Kirk, and he took the stool resting his heels on the lower iron bracket. "A double Old Taylor." When the bartender returned with the order. "Give Dad a drink." The bartender duplicated the old man's order. Kirk put his drink away and pushed it toward the bartender's end for a refill.

"Nice night," said the gray-haired man.

"Every night's nice, Dad, as long as you have money," Kirk said crisply.

"My first time in Chicago in ten years. Came to visit my daughter-in-law." Kirk prepared himself for the picture routine. He wanted nothing of old men or pictures, just activity. The Old Taylor was gone again.

"Are you trying to forget something?"

"No! Just trying to remember something." Kirk pushed back the stool. Walked toward the washroom.

"Good-looking evening," said the attendant, "but those shoes ain't looking so good." Kirk allowed himself to be guided in the shoeshine chair. He followed the drum of the rag, buzzing the tips of the brown shoes, putting on a mirror polish.

"Lookin' for the ladies tonight?" said the bucktoothed attendant, his head bent low and the hand whipping along and not missing a stroke.

"Perhaps."

The shoes were getting glassy.

"I know a friendly girl ... awfully lonesome tonight, too."

"How friendly?"

"Very—very," the deep voice said. The rag moving slower now. "Her name's Jerry."

"Not some bag?" Kirk asked.

"This is delicate stuff. Man, if you see it, you won't renege. She's young, built, and I mean built."

He was brushing Kirk's coat. "Respectable place."

Kirk gave him a dollar. "Keep the change."

The attendant handed him a small piece of paper with a scrawly penciled number on it.

"In case the gentleman changes his mind."

Kirk walked past the bar, didn't look back to see if the old man was still there.

He found his haven in Vanelli's, the bartenders flipping the shakers high, wide and fancy. Putting on the show for the fraternity brothers, in transit or out on the loose. The drinks came faster, and the night time was sand drifting down the glass toward morning.

Kirk was ejected from the rathskeller when he horned in on a German beer-bust party; and all he could remember was the "M.C.," Herr Louie, with three girls from the audience, their backs to the crowd and their escorts, and Louie saying, "Did you ever see three prettier fannies than these?"

Kirk wandered the streets with his feet now a little light, and the night half gone.

Past Van Buren on State Street Kirk stopped to look at a life-size sign in front of a small burleycue. He moved past the sign.

He shoved the thought back in his mind. Tonight, there was an electric crackle in the air, and he could feel the hustle and excitement running along State Street. It was a hurdy-gurdy world made for a young man with whisky under his belt and whorehouse money in his pocket. Kirk fingered the bills, and his other hand twirled the cigar into the gutter.

One doorway pimp called him over. In detail, he described his girl.

"I have a nice little babe tucked away on Harrison Street." He looked Kirk over.

"Any way you want it and no rush." When Kirk hesitated, he kept talking and guiding Kirk around the corner. Entering an old brownstone building with a moth-eaten carpet and the pungent smell of carbolic acid in the hall, Kirk alerted himself. A lone light bulb flickered and cast a dim light. The pimp let him into a door on the second floor.

"Where's the girl?" asked Kirk eagerly. He could hear her heels, and when she entered Kirk felt a dull spot in his stomach. Thirty-five years old if she was a day and near one hundred eighty pounds.

Kirk looked at the pimp and back to her.

The pimp said, "What's the matter?"

"Thought you said she was young?" Kirk said.

"She *is* young," said the pimp angrily.

"Young!" said Kirk. "She was young at the Columbia Exposition."

"Come on," and a metallic eagerness entered the pimp's voice.

"Not me," Kirk said uneasily. "Count me out."

"What do you mean out!" The pimp's voice rose.

"Just what I said."

"If you're not goin', lay some dough on the line. I didn't leave the corner for nuthin'." The whore took Kirk by the arm and attempted to lead him toward the bedroom.

He jerked clear. "Not me."

The pimp put his face near Kirk. "Are you going or not?"

The woman edged closer. "You're not leaving until I get a fin," she said.

"No soap," said Kirk edging toward the door. This was difficult. Kirk knew sometimes they had an extra guy in the place. And it was no use to yell copper. They were all in on the honey.

When the pimp spun him around, he swung. Kirk could hear a bony crack and as his shoulder followed, he felt a pain in his hand. The pimp was on the floor. Eyes dazed. The woman stabbed her fingers at Kirk's face. He ran down the hall, out into the darkened street and a block later he paused.

"Jesus Christ. Two beefs in one night." Kirk

wiped his face. She had only caught him once and the scratch was not deep. Kirk looked at his hand. It was beginning to swell. Not much. He looked at the blinking neon light.

The whisky couldn't come fast enough until the hammers began pounding in his head. Was the trouble with him or Gump or the pimp? What troubles man went through for a woman. He watched the cigarette girl come past the table, the black waitress uniform high in back, showing long, black French seams.

"Give us a cigar."

Kirk placed a dollar on the tray. It disappeared with the girl. Motioning to the waitress, he then fumbled in his pocket.

"The manager said enough."

"Enough, why I ..." Martin's cautioning voice came back to him, avoid beefs like a plague.

Kirk stood and fumbled for some matches, to come up with the wadded paper. He broke into a lopsided smile. The evening could be salvaged. Somehow, somewhere, someone would play. Someone at the end of the wire.

Entering the phone booth he dialed the number.

"Yes."

"Met a friend," Kirk stammered.

"Where at?"

He gave the Wabash joint. The voice gave a number on Roosevelt Road.

"How much?" asked Kirk.

"Don't talk money over the phone." And Kirk was holding the receiver on a dead line. Outside when the air hit him Kirk could feel his liquor. A buzzing inside his head.

The Cadillac made an erratic pattern south, and he drove past the apartment house twice. He saw the blue light thinly disguised on the second floor. The second time around he parked on the off street.

Kirk knew he was rolling, but he had called the cards in the afternoon. Rocks rolled tonight, Marty or not, and the girl better be sharp-looking, he said to himself, as he entered the hall and walked up the steps. Knock three times according to instructions, and a face was peering out at him. She held the door open for him to enter.

"'You?" he asked.

"Goodness no," said the madame, and he was inside the cluttered front room. The blue light cast a ghoulish smoke against the walls. In the corner he could see a makeshift bar. He figured. A place where the finger man works in a downtown joint can't be too dangerous and the madame was friendly.

"Where's the girls?"

"We only got one. She's busy." Her movements were heavy as she walked behind the bar. Jello in all the flavors. The madame had hips able to accommodate the *Tribune* Tower. "Besides, you won't need more than one. Jerry's a mighty popular girl with you young bucks. She'll be here in time. What you goin' to drink?"

Kirk ordered whisky, bought the madame a drink and she only took one dollar from the extended three he had in his hand. No clip joint.

Light tapping on the door and he finished the drink. Already he was woozy and the blue light blurred his vision.

The door opened, and a small compact blonde, the cherubic type, walked in. Her hair, cut short, framed a young unwrinkled face. Not more than twenty, thought Kirk. She smiled, showing even teeth. Her halter brassiere filled adequately and her belly curved.

"You waiting for Jerry?"

Her arm was through his and he smelled the lush odor of Tabu or some similar brand. All the ingredients were there, and he was going to get a bellyful.

The bedroom was less cluttered. The main furniture piece was the bed. "You fix Jerry up and take your clothes off."

"How much?"

"You want a good time, or you're just fooling?"

Kirk tried to refocus, undecided whether to call it off, or make a go; and now in the bedroom, under the white light, he could see the young face, and a nice armful, and the hoppy movement said, "You're for me, honey."

"Ten too much?" she said.

"One time?"

"You go home satisfied."

"No *bull* now." He was fishing in his pocket and pulled out some ones. Not enough. Found a ten down deep. Jerry left the room.

His shirt was off and pants going down when she returned, and behind her a big bruiser. Big, real big. Kirk pulled on his pants. His pulse quickened and the liquor fell into the background.

"A roll job?" he barked.

"This ain't no roll job. And it ain't no foolin' around time either." Kirk could see the broad sweep of the shoulders. He would play hell getting out of here tonight.

"No foolin' around time I said," and the man's voice boomed. He threw the crumpled ten on the bed near Kirk. Kirk's eyes moved from the bill back to the broad shoulders and behind him the girl and the madame.

"We don' want that fake money. What you tryin' to pull?"

Kirk picked the bill, looked at it. "This is no good?"

"You know it ain't no good. Come now, get on that shirt and your goin' to leave fast and better give a tip for Jerry here, a big tip. Another man had entered the room. Shorter, with long arms almost to the floor. Kirk was putting on his shirt, sober now, half expecting a knife and wondering if Martin would find the Cadillac.

"Cough up, or Bruno can get mighty mean."

"No use to be mad about this mistake," said Kirk much soberer now. "I can straighten up."

"You bet ... Look him over." The big one said to the other. The smaller one edged to Kirk and Kirk decided to see this out. No chance in a beef. Maybe he could square it. God! Martin would know what to do. The other searched his pockets, came up with six dollars. And some change.

The big one said, "Give him the change. Now git! And don' ever come back."

So far they had not pushed him around. Even the smaller one going through his pockets was firm in turning him around, but not too rough. Kirk walked out of the bedroom. Carrying his coat. The girl Jerry and the madame stood aside.

"Here, we don't need this." The big bulky man threw the crumpled ten on the floor. Kirk expected the kick as he bent for the bill. There was no kick, only a firm ejection and the closing of the door. He hurried down the stairs to the corner. He turned and looked back. As he approached the Cadillac a thought entered his mind. The keys. Where were the keys? He ruffled his pockets. No doubt the two bouncers would come tearing around the corner. Looking inside the Cadillac he could see them—the keys in the ignition. "Christ, if Martin only knew."

And when the Cadillac turned the corner, he blew a sharp whistle. "Nothing but double trouble all day," Kirk said to himself. The Cadillac leaped to meet the morning sun's trickle of light that touched the macadam.

CHAPTER V

The deposit brought the bank balance to six hundred dollars. One month and the sum total of Kirk's efforts was six hundred tangible cartwheels in a Gary bank, far below his goal. He could discount the everyday living, gambling and clothes, necessities for sure; but he knew he had fallen short of his goal. His goal arbitrarily was two thousand and that wouldn't push his luck too far. When sheaves of phony bills kept turning up at the banks, the Feds would be scouring the city for the plant and passers. One thing he had to do—he had to cut expenses. More trips to the banks and less trips to the night spots. His move of nightly operation was going stale. One month since Martin hit Chicago and so far neither of them had tagged a potential movie star or contest winner. Plenty of floosies around. Things had not changed drastically, just altered a bit.

Today was Martin's pickup day. Kirk didn't know where he got the bills; or how much he received for each bill passed. All Kirk knew was that Martin could always get them and plenty of them. Maybe Marty had two or three fellows *passing*. Kirk calculated Martin's passing less and less. Many days Kirk passed alone in the afternoon, while Marty was at the track.

He placed the wallet in his back pocket and drove the Cadillac back to the city. When he was ahead of the game he would not have to borrow Marty's car.

He had his eye on the '50 Olds convertible model. A pale-green model, similar in color to the Cadillac. But this was playing futures.

Martin was still sleeping. The golf bags, Marty's new kick, stood upright in the corner.

"Sleep all day?" He shook Marty who immediately glanced toward the clock.

"Christ. Why didn't you wake me up earlier?" Martin threw on some slacks, a shirt. Some quick water on his face, and Kirk watched him from the window crossing to the Cadillac, the briefcase in his hands.

Kirk braced his feet on the bed and glanced at the sports section. Yankees in town today. Who would pitch for the Sox? He debated on going to the game or not. His face was losing the tan and he needed the sun. He turned the radio dial. The game had started. If he took a cab, he wouldn't make it before the fourth inning.

The announcer dramatized the details; and by the fifth inning Kirk was asleep.

He ate alone that night in Vito's. The place was alive with customers hovering around the spaghetti and meatballs. Kirk washed his down with a sixteen-ounce schooner of beer. When he looked up, Barney was coming in the door. Barney paused at the bottom of the steps. Kirk's eyes met his. Barney crossed the room.

"Go for a drink?"

"Anything you say."

Barney sipped the Collins across from Kirk. A bantam rooster, thought Kirk, and he could see a few age wrinkles were gathering at the edge of Barney's eyes. "You're looking good, Barney."

"You look like a bit of the same, Kirk. Where's the loot coming from?"

"The horn of plenty. Martin fixed me up with some princess. All I do is wait for the checks," Kirk answered. "I'm taken care of, but well."

"No need for me to tell you about an old friend, then,"

Barney was smiling, showing a blank spot where a tooth should be. "A mutual friend. Closer to you, though."

"Jake in town?"

"Sexier than Jake."

"Not—" Kirk turned the name in his head. "Jeannie?"

"I'll swear her bust is getting bigger. Don't know how the hell they could without her falling forward. You ever get in that, Kirk?"

"No, but I wish I could."

"So does every clown on Sixty-third Street. What she hasn't got, nobody needs."

"Where did you see her?" Kirk could feel Barney's eyes searching his face to sense the opening for a humorous line. Barney was hot on the kidding, a perpetual razzer.

"One more drink and I'm going."

"Where, Barney?"

"Kimbark, and for a slight remuneration I'll tell you where she's working."

"I'd give a twenty to know where."

"Don't have to go for a twenty. Just catch the tab." Kirk paid for the drinks, waited for Barney to give with the information.

"She's working in the *El Conejo* on North Clark Street."

"Not the rat race?"

"It's renovated and under new management."

"I'll bet."

They separated, and after the drink Kirk hurried

to the room. Martin wasn't home and the place was
stuffy. Opening the windows, Kirk kicked over the
golf bag. He let the clubs lie on the floor. Changing
into his blue coat and gray slacks, he took a quick
look into the mirror and was gone. He wondered as
he cleared the steps two at a time. He had never made
the grade with Jeannie but somehow tonight he felt
things would be different.

Kirk could see her name in lights, and on top,
when the cab pulled to a stop. The *El Conejo* was one
of the many strip joints on North Clark Street. Down
close to a small Filipino settlement, its large
Christmasy red and green neon flickered. A red
outlined neon jack rabbit changed shape like a
strobe-image, moving its feet toward the brilliantly
red-lacquered swinging doors. A red and white
striped canopy came flush to the curb; and a
coffee-faced Negro, spangled in what could be
mistaken for an admiral's uniform, hawked the
various names of the headliners and their abilities.
The contrast was like a new Cadillac parked in
among the rusty skeletons of a junkyard. Near the entrance four Filipinos were jabbering. One wore a tan
alpaca coat although Kirk wiped a stream of sweat
from his brow.

Inside whispers of smoke hung like a veil of
opaque gauze. The bar was moved back along the
wall and disappeared into the land of nowhere. Big
splotches of brass along the bar and washroom doors
glowed garishly. Like Barney had said, renovated and
remodeled. The orchestra had stopped playing as the
M.C. entered the spotlight. Kirk glanced at the
half-filled house. He stopped the waitress, slipped her
a dollar bill.

"Get me a front." He followed her. Gave his
order. "What time does the headliner come on?" The

waitress shook her head.

"It's continuous." Her gum snapped.

"Who is she?"

"Who is who?"

"The headliner?" asked Kirk.

"She's a French girl. Jeannie."

"From Paris?" asked Kirk.

"Direct." The waitress winked.

"As French as Barney's newsstand," said Kirk and he looked around the house.

Behind Kirk were the four Filipinos. Kirk recalled the scores of pool halls around the *El Conejo*. The gambling parlors crowded in front with black patent-leather hair. Slicked down for what? There were no Filipino women. He visualized the men standing around appraising their own shoes and the buttocks of passing women. A passion for leather showed in the slick mirror polish of their shoes. The passion for blondes which obsessed them had filled the local movies of Jean Harlow with sloe-eyed patient men. The same drive packed them into the burlesque shows to see stars like Lili St. Cyr.... You would think the St. Cyr gal was Miss Clark Street of 1954. Kirk laughed and in his head was a grotesque picture of the Lili St. Cyr with long legs running in circles, being chased by banty black-haired men with leather shoes.

"Bring another," he ordered the waitress.

Impatiently he walked through the brass-decorated washroom door. Writings marked the walls, obscene symbols of this generation. Kirk remembered Barney's explanation: these scribblings were man's creative and artistic search for his soul. Kirk looked at the words and drawings. In ink, he read: *Chicago is not called the Windy City because of climatic conditions; but because of the violence and verbosity of her citizens.* Over to the left were drawings. Though distorted, the drawings carn their intent. He saw his cigar smoke crawl along the walls, giving the lines a mysterious fluid effect. Pushing the brown stub into the sand-filled stand. Inside he allowed his eyes to adjust to the semidarkness.

The back-stage voice said, "And direct from Paris. The golden haired sensational Jeannie. Give her a hand." The audience responded. The band beat out a fanfare. Kirk looked back where the Filipinos were coming to life.

This was Jeannie, he could catch glimpses of her through the smoke, full-lipped, a coy way with the eyes, and a slow, low-snapped way of the hips. Gone was the carbon-colored hair of Jeannie's. A pinkish gold mass glistened covering her shoulders. Kirk followed her movements as she pranced around the floor. Stopping near the front, speaking in her faked French accent the barrelhouse coming through, she said. "Jeannie will be very naughty tonight." Her tongue flicked out to wet the pursed lips. Rapport ran through the audience. Kirk could see the spectators were no longer passive; they would carry the details home. The golden wavy hair draped over the deep Miami tan of the face; and a flimsy transparent pale blue nightgown around the slow, provocative body. Kirk looked at the other faces along the front row. Attentive faces, liquored faces, looking in at the sex shop. The gown disappeared leaving nothing but red high heels and Jeannie. The varnished tan of the body was only broken by the Bikini suit outlines, leaving pale breasts with inserts like blue bonbons and the alabaster hip area. She held her hand cupped to the ear, listening to the applause. One knee was propped on the satiny large round ottoman in the center of the

lds 'em up?" a voice behind Kirk
Jeannie was on the ottoman, arching her
calves under the mauve tan of the thigh.
y, unbearably slow, with belly twitching, and
rat-a-tat, the big pale buttocks went through the
curtain on the final drum.

Kirk turned his head, one Filipino both hands
deep in the alpaca looked as if he had seen a ghost.
One of the little brown brothers had fallen by the
wayside. Minutes later Jeannie came through the
aisle, her breasts loose in a thin voile dress. Kirk
motioned her to the table.

"Are you alone?" Jeannie asked.

"Why?"

"I saw Martin today in a breezy car. I waved at
him but he didn't see me. Talk around town, you and
Martin hit a gold mine." Her eyes were luminous
even in the smoke-stained room.

"Only talk. We're legit. The horses been paying
off."

"I'm not nosey," Jeannie said. "Have you the
car?"

"No, but I've got cab prices."

Every hour Jeannie went backstage. Did her strip
in a new costume. Came back to the table. Kirk
observed Jeannie's interest in him. He studied her
expressions and for the first time noticed the
awkward way she handled her cigarette. She nibbled
at the tobacco. Then she would search for the loose
bit on her lip. The cigarette stuck in her mouth with
at least three quarters of an inch inside; and when she
puffed Kirk considered the resemblance to a Persian
cat tugging at a tassel. He could feel her knee rub
against his.

"I can ditch my date," Jeannie said.

Things had certainly changed. Kirk was in greenback alley. Everyone was interested: there would be little trouble tonight.

Kirk walked past the stage-door Johnnies. He led the way to the cab. Inside, Jeannie snuggled against his shoulder. The intermediate steps were fast. Some gin, and the cab was alongside a University Avenue curb. The salmon-colored front of the apartment house beckoned and the door opened into an apartment; small, neat, chic. Jeannie's taste in clothes carried over into the apartment.

Kirk threw the package into the chair and their bodies met. Her lips pulled and drew his strength. He could feel the pelvic bones, the round, sweet body crawl against his.

His hands moved inside her dress top feeling the warm skin.

"Let's do this right—and slow." Her lips drawled into an obscene oval.

The lights were off and the disrobing was gradual. One long drink, and the voile dress fell to the floor. Jeannie's lips nibbling and chattering.

"Did you learn this in Miami?" Kirk bolder than ever, pressing his advantage.

"Don't talk," Jeannie murmured.

And his fingers plucked the shoes from her feet. Now Jeannie had control, her lips scorching his until his hands were nervous and jittery fumbling with the buckles and garter belt. Tingling with static electricity as they attempted to rush Jeannie along the now certain road. Transparent, sheer stockings peeled one at a time like plucking the skin from a soft grape. One at a time. Jeannie interrupted with her lips pressed, enveloping his mouth. Until Kirk heard the two pulse beats, coordinated like generators set at a master switch. And she was off the couch.

He tried to say something, her hand covering his mouth. "Get in bed like a good boy." He followed the undulate roll of her hips in silhouette.

The bed covers were down. Kirk rested on an elbow waiting. The beams of the cars would come across the ceiling, and the one street lamp forced its light through the wavering curtains.

He could see her approaching. She floated toward him. He reached up, grabbed her roughly, pulled her down to his side. No perfume here, like the Gold Coast crowd, only a wonderful, fresh, clean womanly smell. Her lips found his ear and her teeth gripped tight.

The disjointed whispers assembled and sent urgency into his arms. Jeannie had her own epileptic dance, angles, abstract angles; and the shadows leaped from the corners, murmuring.

The early gray suede of morning released Kirk from the phantasmagoria. He moved to the kitchen. Jeannie was holding two glasses ready to re-enter the bedroom.

Grabbing her by the waist, he pulled her closer, her body falling against the porcelain table top.

"Kirk!" she admonished. "It's cold."

He pulled her away and their lips met, the glass spilling its cold liquid on his legs. And the wonderful long satin legs wrapped the linoleum, gray suede morning, milkman's rattling bottles, into a mechanical spinning top.

Her teeth marks on his ear and one lip bruised, Kirk said, "Baby, I'm never letting you go."

Three days later they moved to the apartment on Woodlawn. Kirk watched Jeannie slip into a pink summer dress. "Aren't you wearing a brassiere?"

"Don't need one with this."

Kirk stood up to look. The heavy lining and elastic of the dress top held her breasts high and firm.

"I was wondering how you would keep them from bouncing."

When she walked to the dresser he saw the hips swing; even in the house she was burlesque.

"You've never been to a bookie?"

Jeannie shook her head.

"Well, let us go. We can give the gang a treat."

Jeannie twisted the one-carat, fishtail diamond around her finger. Kirk eyed his gift, one hundred down, the rest in nice easy payments. They walked out of the apartment.

Metzner's bookie had a cigar store front. But inside through a loosely guarded door was the medium-boxed room. The large markup sheets dangled decorously, and as Hutch would remark frequently, Metzner's was a poor man's Wall Street. Red leather and chrome chairs were filled, still many were standing. The vapid, vacuous stares of the gamblers. Fat blustery women, nervous toe-tapping men, mousy clerks, only gave a passing glance to Jeannie as Kirk escorted her through the door. Kirk knew that gamblers made poor jumps, their sex drive completely subordinated to a gambling urge that gnawed their organs like a cokey's wish. A small black and white terrier sat impassively near a lopsided woman. Kirk remembered her before his stretch up the river. Her stringy hair and the face impassive as the dogs, a prefrontal lobotomy face. The fan rippled the markup sheets. And the line formed at the cubicle window, and Metzner's money man, green eyeshade and all, scribbled calligraphic figures on the small cards.

"Who are you betting on?" Jeannie asked.

"The Brass Monkey."

"Let me make the bet."

"Here." He gave her two dollars. Jeannie went to the short line.

"Hey, Doyle."

Doyle's face looked miniature, overpowered by the horn-rimmed glasses. He had on his seedy gray sweater hung over a pair of heavy work pants. He had a book in his hand.

"What are you reading?" Kirk took the book from Doyle. The title was *The Function of the Orgasm* by Wilhelm Reich.

Kirk scratched his head. "You'll never find a winner in there."

Jeannie came back with the tickets. Kirk watched Doyle's face turn white.

"What's the matter?"

"Nothing," Doyle said. His fingers shook as he took the book from Kirk.

"Are you sure?"

"I have a cold, and I'm not supposed to be out."

"A cold in summer?"

"Sure, silly," Jeannie said.

"Doyle, do you know Jeannie?"

"We've never met."

"Jeannie, Doyle. Doyle, Jeannie."

"I better go."

Doyle touched his hat, and moved out of the doorway.

"He's a queer duck," Jeannie said.

"But smart."

"In that sweater?"

"There are different ways of being smart," Kirk said.

"I like your way best," she answered.

"What did you mean by that?"

"I'm not so dumb myself," Jeannie said.

Kirk watched the housewives, some standing with groceries, blowing the old man's dough and relief checks. Everybody was broke; but you would never know it at Metzner's. Yeh! When the rustle of green bills was heard all the vultures came flying.

"Are you talking to yourself?" Jeannie asked.

"Why?"

"Your lips were moving."

"I'm saying a prayer. For the Brass Monkey."

The loudspeaker blurted, "And here comes the Brass Monkey between horses gaining ground—There in the stretch, Brass Monkey and Profile—The Brass Monkey is drawing clear."

Jeannie's hand was holding his elbow. Her eyes glistened.

Kirk bit his lip. He tore a wrapper from a cigar, jammed it in his mouth, tilted it at a cocky angle.

"A big shot," said Hutch the board man.

Kirk watched Hutch shift his eyes from the cigar to Jeannie.

The voice was heard over the loudspeaker. "Get your bets in for the fifth race. We're going to have a raid."

"What do we do?" Jeannie asked.

"Nothing. Just watch the people."

Everyone moved easily. Kirk had Jeannie make another bet. When they moved out of the place, Kirk saw Hutch putting the chrome and red leather chairs into the backroom. He would replace them with old wooden hard-backed chairs. Kirk watched some people go into Hencke's for a hot-dog. Others went for a beer or to the pool hall. But most people stayed on the sidewalk around the corner. Jeannie had her hand in his. Not nervous. This was a big joke. A God-damned big joke. Kirk held the cigar idly and waited.

First the sound of sirens and then the wagon
pulled up. The bluecoats poured out. They had to be
dramatic. Photographers were with them. Inside, the
fireworks began. Kirk could hear the axes at work.
The law was breaking up the furniture. The moldy
old   wooden   chairs   were   being   knocked   to
smithereens. Everyone on the sidewalk knew Metzner
had many of these chairs. Enough to satisfy many
more raids. More noise inside, and the photographers
getting their pictures.

In a few minutes the police re-emerged. They had
one figure between them. Hutch. The same old story.
Down to the station. Bail. And Hutch would be back
on the markup board for the seventh race. The
photographers carried on the joke and snapped
pictures, the store front, and the assembled people.

Tomorrow Metzner's bookie on the front page.
Day after, some other bookies, and after that *East
Lynne*. Chicago was getting more virtuous every day.

The commotion subsided and the paddy wagon
pulled away with the ignoble Hutch. Kirk watched
the crowd go back into the bookies.

The help would be sweeping out the vestiges of the
raid and the chrome and red leather chairs would be
back in place.

"Now what, Kirk?" Jeannie asked.

"We can pick up the winners later, if we have
one."

Kirk held her arm waiting to cross the street.

Tomorrow morning, Kirk knew, the papers would
spread the raid, front-page center. But in the bookie
everything would be the same. Except now, the
temporary absence of Hutch.

Kirk looked back. Doyle was standing along the
wall of the Tower Apartments. His body was
half-hidden by a car, and his eyes were following

them.

CHAPTER VI

Kirk braced the newspaper on the steering wheel, and recognized the remorse that bordered on anxiety and fear. Gump and Roy were dead. No names were mentioned in the newspaper, but he didn't need names, the descriptions being deadly and accurate. One blind man and an oversized gray-black haired giant had tapped a can of wood alcohol in Jackson Park. The vision of Roy and Big Gump lying face down at the edge of the football field, overpowered Kirk. He took account of himself, listening to the splatter of the summer raindrops, tapping like a blind man's cane on the car's tin roof. A feeling of remorse over the last argument with Gump lay deep in his stomach like a ball of clay. The raindrops were stopping, and now gently, lightly, until the air was restive and still. In the distance, a rainbow framed like a dome the black girders of a newly erected building. It was time to start passing again.

Kirk finished his last pass. Eighteen bills in one day. Not enough, but he was tired. And all morning since the newspaper information his nerves had been jumpy. Kirk calculated Martin's earlier exaggeration. They were to make a killing. Someone was making it in this racket. Kirk was sure he wasn't the one. Martin always had cash, he recalled. Marty talked plenty but never about money. Kirk tried to guess at Martin's cut. He didn't know. Also Marty didn't have his expenses. One charge account for Jeannie last month: three hundred dollars. This was the law of diminishing returns. Jeannie would have to settle for less; or he would have to start passing earlier. No

shaking off a binge at noon. He remembered one day
last month he had shoved fifty-two bills in one day.
Up and down, double back, that's what was
necessary. One month like that or say one hundred a
day. Two grand. And they would move on. Chicago
was getting worked out; and luck doesn't hold out
forever. If Jeannie stopped the spending spree maybe
they could leave at the end of summer. Marty wanted
to go to New York. So did he. He would sound out
Jeannie about the trip. Kirk thought of the past five
weeks with Jeannie. Jeannie was a bedroom artist, no
doubt about that. He remembered the notches he had
made on the bedroom door one night. Six notches
that night. Kirk eased the rented Ford through the
traffic. How long could a guy keep a machine like
that? Kirk wondered. What happens to me when I
conk out or run short of dough. He pushed the
thoughts from his mind. Unconsciously he passed
through a red light.

When he entered the apartment, Jeannie was
standing by the full-length mirror holding a black lace
dress in front of her. She had nothing on, only high
heels.

"How does it look?"

"Your fanny looks wonderful."

"How about the dress?"

"Expensive." He looked around. Boxes spilled all
over the room. Carson's, Field's and other Michigan
Avenue shops. He watched Jeannie place the dress
over the couch. Her bare, smooth body moved to
another box. Jeannie loved clothes, but only for the
outside. Whenever she came indoors, at work or their
apartment, off with the clothes. He recalled her
making breakfast, a small apron of a half yard of
material, nothing else. And her passion for the mirror.
The full-length mirror had set him back twenty bucks.

One day's passing so Jeannie could admire her frame.

"What goes with the clothes?"

"Remember, you said we should take a vacation. Well, I told the boss we were planning to get hooked, so he gave me a week off for the honeymoon."

"Christ, why didn't you do it up right and get a bridal veil."

Jeannie passed her left hand by his face, her kewpie lips twisted into a smile.

Kirk looked at her hand. A diamond wedding-ring had been added to the big sparkler. Jeannie had never discussed marriage. Jeannie never discussed anything. Like Doyle her personality was complicated. The years he had spent in prison were blanks on Jeannie. Whenever he asked how she had become a stripper, she fenced with words and then an endless chatter. When he pursued too close, too many questions, her hands would flutter, and then the heat would be on, smoldering heat, melting into a crucible of steel that ended in the epileptic dance that was the salve for all wounds. Another blank page was the Otis-Miami deal. Where was Otis? What had become of the camera modeling? How did she acquire the job at the *El Conejo?* Why the taffy blonde hair? Questions to end in an epileptic dance to end all questions? He had left well enough alone. Except the pressure upon him to get rings. Her pitch was: people see us coming in and out of the apartment. Should I get a ring. *Should* meant *would* in her lingo.

"Have you been wearing the ring at work?"

"Yes."

"While stripping?"

"The boss said I should. It does something to certain kinds of men. The older ones, he said."

"From now on take the rings off. All those jerks see me pick you up."

"My, you're getting jumpy lately. If you want me to, I will. Now watch." Jeannie pulled a green bathing suit from the papers.

Kirk looked at the skimpy suit. Even holding it in front of her, it didn't cover much.

"You might as well go out as you are, as wear that."

"It's the new style."

She jumped in his lap, rumpled his hair.

"Now don't be mean. We have a week off and we can go down to the beach and some of the ritzy joints you always talked about."

"Those clothes cost money." Kirk picked up the suit and looked at the label.

"It's from France," Jeannie said. "You want me to look good, don't you? Anyway, I said I would throw all of my money in every week."

Kirk remembered her offer. He had never expected it. Yet, Jeannie's money and his would never cover their brand of living. Clothes, liquor, cigars, dinners, belted the hell out of his small pile. She kissed him, open mouth. Her tongue explored the inside of his lip. He lifted her up and moved toward the bedroom.

"No. Wait, Kirk. Not now."

"Why not?"

"You said the other night that we would drive out to the dunes today."

"Did I?"

"Don't you remember?"

"I'll have to check out a car."

"No, you won't." Jeannie walked to her purse. She stood there swinging the Cadillac keys on her fingers.

"Where did you get those?"

"Martin. I told him about my days off and he thought it was a good idea to use the Cadillac."

"When did you see him?"

"Downtown this morning. He drove me home."

"He sure does get around. Who mentioned the Cadillac first?"

"I did. And he saw it my way."

The Cadillac crossed from Indiana into Michigan. Kirk's spirits were better. Jeannie was kneeling on the seat beside him, her arm around his neck. He could feel the rub of her fingers along the hairs on his neck. A bottle of sloe gin was on the floor in a paper bag. Jeannie's suggestion. And in his pocket was seventy dollars of her money. She had stuck by her offer.

"I like the smell of your cigar."

"You should. It is a Corona."

"What is that?"

"A foreign cigar."

"And you're kicking about my suit."

Kirk patted her knee. The road was empty and he followed a sign. Five miles to the beach. The car had a sense of power. Kirk liked to stroke the wheel and a slight push on the foot would jump the car. Ahead, he could see the blue of the water. Below the July sun it was hot. The car moved into a clump of trees. Kirk pulled it out of sight from the road. He was careful not to drive the wheels into soft sand. The beach was bare. And behind them the dunes rolled inland like small hills.

He followed Jeannie from the car and watched her feet shift in the sand. She had on white slacks and a blue flannel coat. Her heavy blonde hair crept from under a yachting cap. She was carrying the green suit in her hand.

"Where are we going to change?" he asked.

She looked around. Her eyes moved down the beach and back to the big dune hill.

"Can't we find a place behind that, facing the sun? I need a tan."

Kirk helped her up the dune. And on the other side they found a clear spot; surrounded by the peak of the dune, with trees on the other side. The sun baked into the sand. While he was putting the blanket down, he felt the sweat running from under his arms.

"This is sheltered. No one can see us here, can they, Kirk?"

He looked around. They were up from the beach and the trees sheltered the other side. Jeannie was sitting on the blanket, and the sandals and blue flannel coat were off.

He fingered his cigar.

"Go ahead. Smoke your cigar. I'll have a cigarette."

He felt her fingers steady his hand as she lit her cigarette from the cigar. He then took the sweatshirt and wiped the sweat from his forehead and chest. Jeannie had the white blouse off. Kirk looked around.

"No one can see. Isn't it all right?"

"Sure." He looked at the breasts, then their eyes met and they grinned at each other.

Kirk watched the heat waves dance from the sand. And the day was still. Only the splash of waves pounding the shore moved into the quiet hollow. Underneath, the blanket was hot and their clothes were piled on end. When Jeannie took a drink from the sloe gin, a trickle rolled down her chin and dropped to her breast. The suntan oil was out.

"Put some on, Kirk."

His hand followed the curves of her body and the oil was sticky. The sloe gin and heat were beginning to affect him.

"All done."

Jeannie stood up. She wiggled her hips at him. He

watched her leap around mimicking the ballet dancers. His arm reached out, caught her leg. She fell down.

The heat moved around, and in between them. Kirk felt the sun scorching his back, and the sticky oil on Jeannie mingled with their sweat. They rolled and her back was on the hot sand, only her legs still on the blanket. The sand burned Kirk's elbow. Still Jeannie said nothing. He drew his face up for one second. Jeannie's eyes were closed; and her mouth twisted, full lips leaping to encompass his.

When he awoke the sun was beginning to dip. Jeannie was above him, shaking him, and he saw that the sloe gin was almost gone. Her pupils contracted in the brutal sunlight, her hair was tangled and messed with sand. She dropped to her knees, the gold bands of the rings burned as she stroked his chest.

"Are we going in the water?" she asked.

"We should to wash off."

Jeannie put on the green suit. They walked down the dune. When they were close to the water, Kirk saw one house down the beach partially obscured by trees. The waves were higher, booming against the beach. Jeannie was running, steps uneven. Her knees were in the water. He thought of the almost empty bottle. Before he could call, her figure disappeared. His heart was pounding and his legs picking up a new energy, leaped across the water. He could feel the undertow pull and tug at his legs, and he moved ahead to the spot where Jeannie had disappeared.

The tow had him and his toes tried to grip and feel the sand. As he went under, Kirk's body curled into a ball and he rolled outward. The tow shook his head, and his ears rang. His lungs pounded for air. He could feel the tow releasing him and his legs were out, driving for the top, his arms jarring out against the water. Air was coming, he could sense the surface, getting lighter. His head shot from the water.

When his lungs filled, he looked to the right. Jeannie's face panicky, arms splashing, eyes wide. He saw the hair disappear below the surface. He moved in circles, swimming fast over the area. He looked down but the water below was too muddy. When Jeannie came up again her eyes were closed; her arms had no movement. She was five yards away. She was going under. Her hair bobbing on the surface, and then down. Kirk pushed tired arms, his eyes following the shadows under the water. Legs kicked heavily. He saw her suspended, body straight up, dropping slowly. His arms reached out, missed her. He maneuvered his body. This was the last stab. The air was bubbling in his mouth; he could feel the cold water enter. He grabbed once more for the down-moving head. His fingers locked in the strands of hair. Her body had a gray quality, dirty, muddy, like the mousy underbelly of a trout. His left hand broke the surface.

With air in his chest, legs, arms aching he pulled for the distant beach. He tried to carry her breast-fashion. Her dead weight drove against his hip; and she almost slipped from his grip. Then the head carry. Jeannie's weight became heavier, pulling against the arm muscles. Kirk doubted if he could make the beach. Drop Jeannie, his fogged mind thought. But his fingers locked in her hair and her body towed behind him. Her face bobbed under the water. His arm moved methodically. Thoughts running through his mind. Panic. Then strength; and his fingers were interlocked and numb in Jeannie's hair.

One foot touched the sand.

On the beach his index finger crammed into her throat. Jeannie's face was a pale green. If the *El Conejo* front row could see her now. He had her coughing, vomiting. Face down in the sand. Kirk sat on her legs. Pushing his hands into her side. A breeze rattled his backbone. His steady movements brought a gasping breath. Like a dead fish, and the lips weren't full and rich, but blue from the cold. The hair was matted seaweed, and the body cold and goose-pimpled. When her breathing deepened, she stirred. Kirk carried her to the car.

"Oh! God," her voice cracked.

He placed her in the back seat, ran back for the clothes, blankets and bottle. He forced the bottleneck into her mouth. He could feel her body take the gin.

When the car was on the highway, Jeannie said, "Martin won't like the wet seat."

"The hell with Martin."

The drive back was recklessly fast. Kirk gunned the throttle, begged for speed.

"I want to come up in front."

He stopped the car by a hamburger stand. Jeannie's body was lighter as he lifted her to the front seat. The stand sold hot coffee. They sat in the car feeling the scalding liquid.

"I won't forget this, Kirk."

"Neither will I." And when he said it, he didn't know what it meant or why. He did know that one small grip of the fingers was all that had brought Jeannie back to the beach. He tightened the left hand and felt the tired muscles and wrist. The hand that had saved Jeannie from joining Roy and Gump, he thought. Deaths came in series of three. Had he cheated fate? He started the motor.

Inside the apartment, Jeannie in bed sleeping, Kirk

lay on the couch. Crushed in the bottom of Jeannie's blue flannel coat, he had found another letter. The green ink like the green water and pallor of her cheeks. Addressed to Jeannie at the *El Conejo*. Postmarked September 6. Two days old. This was like getting a shotgun full blast. Pellets coming from all directions: charge accounts, Martin's Cadillac, the sun dance, the struggle with the tow, and now the letter. Jeannie certainly made life interesting. His brain was numb trying to grab a straw, float along, keep his head up. Two months later, the bastard still sending letters. Kirk pulled the pages from the envelope. He looked at the last, forty-one pages. Even longer than the other.

When he read the letter, the day began to be relived. Africa, along the Sahara. Jeannie lost on the sand. A stranger, the writer, finding her. Four pages on a theory of how heat and the sun works into the animal fibers of the brain. As Kirk read, it was as if he were watching a drama played that afternoon. The word *sybarite* again. He remembered Martin had used that word. But this couldn't be Marty. Martin was too fast, hit and run. No three or four hours in a room composing letters. Whoever it was, Jeannie was his dream-girl, a symbol of all women. Unconsciously he hesitated at another new word. *Caryatid*. It had some reference to her shape.

Something had to be done about these letters. Find the goofy bastard. Find out why Jeannie kept them. Kirk began to see ideas. They came together. The mirror, her jobs, walking around the house nude. He would think things over; but something had to be done.

CHAPTER VII

Kirk turned the key in the door. He entered smiling. His face was flushed. Martin was on the couch. Jeannie was looking at her wrist-watch. Her dress was wrinkled.

"Eight o'clock," she said.

Kirk watched her back hand pushing the hair up from her neck, fluffing it. His eyes moved to a new costume pin near her shoulder. Her eyes were on him now. Face puzzled, feline. Kirk could see that Martin had moved to the kitchen to mix drinks. Walking over to Jeannie, Kirk passed at her lips. She turned her face.

"You're drunk," she said.

"So are you," he answered.

Martin brought in the drinks. Jeannie looked at Kirk half-wavering, his feet unsteady. Her lips parted and he could follow the grin and dimple, watch them grow into a smile. Her arm was around him, kissing him.

"How do you like this?" She fingered the pin on her dress.

"What is it, a foetus?" asked Kirk.

"No, silly. It's a sea-horse. Martin bought it for me."

"Martin!"

"I told him I liked sea-horses and he picked one up downtown."

"Obliging, isn't he?" asked Kirk.

"I think so, and I wish you were more thoughtful," Jeannie added.

"The next thing he'll be paying the rent."

"Cut it," Martin interrupted. "Sit down. We can all have a drink."

Kirk slid into the chair, pushing his hand over

Martin's. "No bull! Marty, when are we getting out of town? This dump's getting on my nerves."

"Drink up to our good luck," Martin clicked the glasses. "The business is leaving for New York." He winked at Kirk. "Is Jeannie going with us?"

"You bet," answered Kirk.

"It depends," Jeannie interjected.

"Depends on what?" Kirk's voice had a liquor crackle to it.

"On the drinking. You've been drunk the last two weeks. Spoiled our vacation, and all."

"Why don't we enjoy ourselves? Argue tomorrow after breakfast," Martin said.

"That's good by me." Kirk saw Jeannie smile.

"Martin was going to tell me about his trip to Mexico City. Before he came back to Chicago," Jeannie said.

Kirk watched the cigar smoke creep around Martin's head and give the illusion of a halo.

"Keep talking, Marty. Don't let me interrupt." He turned to Jeannie. "Don't you have to go to the *El Conejo?*"

"I have an hour."

Martin poured another drink. He began. "I ended in Mexico City last year."

"You never told me about that," Kirk said. He added a lopsided wink.

"What's Mexico City like?"

Kirk noticed Jeannie's interest. The liquor was stimulating that rolling belly.

"A piece of rotten wood, painted over with gold paint. Last year they were stealing babies, little babies."

"You're kidding, Marty," Jeannie laughed. "What do they do with them?"

"Sell them. And the ones they couldn't get rid of,

they sold to the chili parlors. One day in a small restaurant, we found a small fingernail in the chili."

"Oh! Martin," Jeannie gasped.

"Don't get gory," said Kirk.

"You want me to tell the truth, don't you?" asked Martin.

"Tell me the truth by all means," Kirk said reaching for the bottle, almost empty.

"I'm down in this hole of the world for a week," said Martin. "Making a hit with the residents. Driving a big Buick and throwing money around like water. Still plenty left, though.... And I run into this broad, what a character. Norma is her name. And this piece of unjelled protoplasm has an uncle, some general who's her patron saint. You know how they are. All jazzed up. Well, this piece of dust talks me into getting a house in the exclusive district. Everything's going along swell. I'm layin' the broad and even get to meet the Mexican general. When I flash a roll he says a nice young man would go far. Mind you I don't get the drift of all their conversation. All I know is, as long as I have the dough I'm kingpin. So one day she talks me into taking the money out of the bank. We're going to run away, escape from the uncle and all. Remember this kid is taking care of me. Like I've never been taken care of before. What she didn't know in the bedroom wasn't necessary. Between the heat, liquor and her I'm groggy. So I go for the deal. I draw all the money out of the bank. I figure we can make the border in two days, and then hit the Mardi Gras in New Orleans. So Norma and I end up in the room. Our place. This exclusive apartment.

"But I'm not stupid. The money's under my pillow along with a forty-five. I'm not trusting these spics. Norm's square I figure, but the general I have my doubts about him. So when I dozed off, I hear Norma moving around. I feel under the pillow. The money still there and the gun. The next thing I know she's gone. So I figure frig her. Tomorrow I take the money and head back to L.A. I bolt the door and go back to sleep.

The next morning, I wake up groggy. A splitting headache. The room's fuzzy, smells of chloroform. And I remember. *The Chloroform Bandits.* I check the pillow. Empty as Lincoln's chair. No gun, no dough. I check the door, unlatched. Outside, no Buick. I dress and head for the general's shack. No general. Does anybody know of him? What general? No general lives here. You must have wrong street. So I try police headquarters. Describe them. Mention the chloroform. They say, too bad. Will try to find. They have no leads. I should have known better. And all that type pass the buck. I end up writing for dough to Hollywood. Never again in that burg."

"That's rich, Martin," said Jeannie and she rose to get dressed.

"You've led an interesting life," said Kirk.

Jeannie re-entered the room. Her heels making her taller and above that nothing but a wisp of silk covering from her waist. The breast bare and pinnacled, uncovered.

"Did you pick up the dress from the cleaners?" she asked.

Kirk looked at her. "Jesus Christ. Get some clothes on." He pointed his thumb toward Martin. "We're not alone."

"So what! He sees this much at the *El Conejo*," she said.

"Get in there."

Jeannie backed into the bedroom. Just her head emerged from the door. "Did you get the dresses?"

"No."

"Kirk," she exclaimed. "You promised."

Kirk watched her disappear again into the bedroom. "Why don't you go easy on the jug," Marty said as Kirk poured himself a stiff shot.

"Why don't you?" Kirk said.

"Don't be wise, the game is getting close."

"What do you mean?" Kirk stretched full length on the couch.

"The Treasury men picked up a passer."

"Are the *headhunters* on our trail?"

"We're in the clear. Only I say be careful. Liquor loosens you, Kirk. You were able to handle the stuff."

"I still can." Inside he was woozy, but if he rose to pace the floor, and tried to work off the alcoholic fog, Marty would know. "Everyone has a crutch. Liquor, women, gambling. What's your crutch, Marty? You haven't gambled for a couple weeks."

"How do you know?"

"The gang at Metzner's and the barbershop said so."

"I've been out at the track. Washington Park's open."

"We'll be out."

"To check?"

"No, I need some fresh air."

"Stay out of the bars," Martin said. "And you can get some."

Kirk watched the cocky tilt of the panatella. But Martin's features were becoming fuzzy. No liquor, no gambling, no women, no vices. Martin was businesslike, but somewhere there would be a flaw. Kirk's head began to throb. He looked at Martin again. In a few minutes when Jeannie emerged ready for work, he made a valiant attempt to rise. One valiant attempt to follow the brown form-fitting jersey dress. A brown jersey stole was wrapped carelessly over her shoulders. The horsetail hairdo bounced. He heard Martin say, "I'll drive you to work." Kirk was too tired to rise.

The door slammed behind them.

When he woke up three hours later, the apartment was dark and silent. Jeannie had departed too easy. No argument about taking her to the *El Conejo*. Martin or the letter-writing dream boy. Something was fishy. He double-locked the door.

Under the bed he found Jeannie's trunk. It was locked. For a few minutes he sweated over the lock. The icepick from the kitchen did the job. He sat on the bed, a cigar jammed between his teeth, and went through the trunk. It was loaded with pictures: nude shots of Jeannie, strip-shots and doubles taken with men by the camera girls in the nightclubs. Then packaged and filling over a quarter of the trunk were the letters. He looked at the dates and envelopes. Some dated back to when she worked for Carson's one summer. Others had been sent to the Rainbow, and many to the Idle Hour and the *El Conejo*. Some asked for dates. Others worked angles. Like letters from hairdresser shops or art studios. Even a letter from a South American business man who had seen her act. Would she work in his club and all that sort of crap. Set aside, tied together with a ribbon, were the ones in green ink. Mister Anonymous had been with Jeannie a long time.

Kirk worked the cigar butt between his teeth. His feet propped on the bed, he went through the entire series. These must be Jeannie's art treasures. He noticed the small penciled definitions of the highbrow words. The pencil writing was in Jeannie's hand. She had also underlined some sections. Velvet rugs and drugs for lasting power. One letter, some fifty pages, all about whips. It was as if he had opened a new mirror upon her. There were thirty-two of these green-ink letters. How could Jeannie keep this crap? He remembered her saying all the strippers received fan mail. What a fan this one was. He grew up with her. Some of the letters were postmarked back as far as the high school days, before her job at Carson's. She had lived a long time with these. Some as long as forty pages. Pieces of tripe. But a hell of a lot the guy said was true and Jeannie practiced much of the stuff. Whether she picked this up from the letters or the goons around those arty shops or West Madison gumbos or that Rush Street crowd, he did not know. But one thing he did know, after coming in contact with her. If she was buggy on her shape or even these letters he had never wanted to lose out. It had been like going to bed with the Kohinoor Diamond or an electric egg-beater. Kirk threw the letters into the trunk and walked down toward Sixty-third. The letters had excited his curiosity.

Kirk entered Vito's to satisfy the empty hungry feeling. The slab of roast beef was tender enough to separate with a fork. He could overhear someone in the next booth talking about the deaths of Roy and Big Gump. An exciting fact would be bandied around the neighborhood for years. Maybe his death, if the *headhunters* came too close. Mentally, he decided that never again would he allow himself to be cooped behind bars. Using the bread slicer as a pusher, he sopped up the gravy. Barney would be in, this was his hangout. The smell of beer and sawdust entered his nostrils. Kirk leaned back, the large cigar he had saved for dinner between his teeth. The long fingers spread the cigar-band on the table. Ramon Allone, No. 1. Sixty cents for the delectable Havana. The little brown-skinned neighbors in Cuba worked ten hours daily over the cigar boards. The quick fingers would mold the wrapper around the fat pack. Maybe their dreams about the cockfights, their escape measures, helped put a unique expressiveness in the cigar. Jeannie said he was crazy. Sixty cents for a cigar. But she thought nothing about putting that rump of hers in twenty-dollar panties.

Barney came down the steps. The abnormally short legs followed by a jockey's barrel chest. He walked toward the table.

"Just the man I want to see." Kirk motioned to the seat. "Two beers, waiter," he said.

"In trouble?"

"No, puzzled."

They sat in back with the two glasses of draft beer. Kirk spoke. "What kind of people are the ones who send horny letters to people?"

"Degenerates."

"Dangerous?"

"Some. The women turn them in; they all get caught sooner or later."

"What if the girl don't turn them in?"

"They don't get caught. Keep on writing." Barney pushed his hat back farther. "Some of these goddam women get a buzz out of this. Even grow fat on it. Why?"

"Oh, I was reading a book."

"Yeh, there's a lot of queer jokers in this world. Do you know the other night some guy stole a manikin out of Fox's window? Didn't touch the fur coats. Just took the plaster doll."

"Them things are six foot tall."

"I know, I know. That shows you. Still everyone's a little queer deep down in their souls."

"And you, Barney?"

"Hundred-dollar bills," Barney answered. "I like

to take a bath in hundred-dollar bills. No water. Just the bills."

Kirk stepped from the cab at Congress and State Street. He would follow the deal through. No use leaving strings untied, he reflected.

He brushed his way through the crowd. All the honky-tonkers lost on the hapless pavements of Chicago. A fire engine clanked by, winked a red light.

The brittle lights from the pawnshops cast an eerie glow on the sidewalk, reflected from the cheap cut glass and fishing reels. The burlesque barkers trying to drag in the uninitiated to see the fat-pork babes of South State. Hustle-bustle, people moving in the cross tide, above the city's din, the clatter of the El competing with the crippled newshawks. Kirk turned into one of the shooting galleries. There were pinball and test-your-strength machines in front. Two sailors guffawed as another tilted a machine. Kirk wandered between the mechanical contrivances. The girlie machines were in back, in a room separate from the other. Kirk changed some bills to dimes and walked to the closest machine.

They were the machines that showed the small dime and nickel movies. Each reel started with: This is for art students only. Art students, Kirk ruminated. The kind the city psychiatrists deal with. The so-called art students the bulls find lodged on some fire escape or hanging over a transom.

Kirk systematically went down the line. Discounting the machines after one reel or sticking it through. Mostly old hay-bags. He moved down the street until he found what he wanted. A small place. The girls in the reels young, fresh, voluptuous. Ten cents a copy. This was not for the stiffs. He found Jeannie on the fifth machine. Fourth reel. No mistaking her. Busty, coy. Smiling, wetting her lips. Always turning in time. Never the hole card. Skillfully done and sexy. Kirk's forehead was wet with sweat. His hands squeezing.... And then the next. Some character went through twice. Kirk stroked his cigar angrily, waited for his turn. In time, eight reels of Jeannie posing on a rock, in a studio on a divan. When Kirk turned from the machine he was confronted. A scarecrow in a green-striped suit. Saggy at the bottom, held up by toothpicks, an ancient leer on his face.

"We got more. Better," said the scarecrow, his cigarette rolling in his mouth half-wet.

"Of her?" said Kirk, motioning to the last machine. The scarecrow's thumbs were hooked in a changer like the streetcar conductors wear.

"Some," he answered, "and better."

"Where?" asked Kirk.

"Up there," said the scarecrow, pointing to a door. "One buck to get in. Bring your own quarters."

Kirk speculated, finally dug deep and bought his way in. He walked up the stairs with forty quarters jingling in his coat pockets.

He had to accustom himself to the dark second floor. As his eyes adjusted, he could see men walking from machine to machine. The machines were against the wall and after one stepped into view of the machine he would be in the truly dark. No part of the dim blue light entered the small cubic area. Wonderful businessmen, these larks, he ruminated.

He tried the same system. These were rough. No hit or miss. He found Jeannie. The reels were clearer and started easy. A keyhole idea. This was Jeannie now entering her bedroom in street clothes. Disrobing, nothing to guess at, no turning away. Everything visible. No wonder the letter-writer knew

Jeannie. She was all here, nothing to guess at. Simulating a love act. Heavy breathing, constant wetting of the lips, squirming. All she needed was a man in the reel. But the imagination could fill in the blanks. All the cheap misguided drips. If they couldn't take your money in the strip shows, dance halls or whorehouses, they worked the second decks. One could have his sex without body contact.

Kirk turned. Over one machine was a small sign. He looked. *Special of the Month. Paris Love Potion.* He stepped into the shadow. The quarter slipped silently into the slot. The film was in color. A dark-haired bartender was at a short bar. One patron, an older man, flabby and fat, sipped a drink. He pantomimed conversation to the bartender. A flash caption said: *Any girls?* He drew a sinuous line with his hands. He wanted a woman. The bartender moved close, pointed to someone who had entered. Kirk braced his forehead against the metal eye rim. This was Jeannie again. A small beret covered the heavy brown hair. The blouse was sheer, she had nothing underneath. A tight red skirt. No stockings and the heels were high and black. Kirk inserted another quarter. And in the next two sequences the plot was obvious. As Jeannie went to the girl's room the patron made a deal with the bartender. Money exchanged hands, and the bartender showed him a bottle labeled love potion. He dropped a few drops in Jeannie's drink before she returned. The patron left. Jeannie was talking to the bartender. Caption. *This man will be troublesome. Can you give him something.* She placed some money on the bar. The bartender had another bottle. Label ... Desexer. Kirk figured, was Mr. Otis the dreamer of this plot? How had Jeannie fallen for this corn? Another quarter. As the drinks progressed, and as each one turned his

head, the bartender would drop a few drops, winking
at the other partner in crime. By the third drink, the
patron became shy modest. And Jeannie became
sensuous, twisting as if on a hot seat, until the beret
and blouse were gone. She stood in front of the man
crawling close, and the bartender google-eyed poured
the entire love potion into her drink. Scene eight
coming up. Another quarter. Three to go. The patron
ran from the bar. Then the skirt dropped to the floor,
Jeannie wiggling like a sex-starved animal. Kirk
promised himself some fast whiskies on this. This
upper room was for the suede shoe boys from out of
town. Someone was being paid off for this. She dangled her finger mischievously at the bartender. The
come-hither finger. Another caption. *Have to call my
wife*. The camera followed the bartender to the phone
and his return, Jeannie stretched flat on the bar. Her
finger crooked again to the bartender. *THE END*.

Kirk gritted his teeth. Everyone had his price, a
trip to Miami and a few promises had put Jeannie
into his corn. Someone was waiting for the machine.
Kirk had been conscious of him earlier. Another of
Jeannie's many admirers. He stepped from the
machine to give the person the place ... The man
brushed his sleeve in the dim blue light. Kirk looked
up. The face was familiar, horn-rimmed glasses. The
cap. Sweater. The man was moving fast. Kirk heard
his steps, two, three at a time. He shouted after him.

"Doyle!"

When he looked down the steps, he saw the gray
sweater disappear from view. Kirk moved after him.
The street was crowded, and no Doyle. He walked in
the direction the man had taken, peering in the
restaurants, hot-dog shacks, arcades. No Doyle. He
stopped on the sidewalk as if dazed. His hand was on
his chin. Could he have been mistaken? He tried to

reshape the body structure, face, glasses. It was a blank wall. Many people looked like Doyle. And what was Doyle doing in one of these peepshows? Kirk scratched his head. The cigar had gone stale. He watched the people's faces, leering, some vacant. Their bodies moved in separate rhythm like sleepwalkers or cokies. He listened to the traffic noises and barkers' voices. All for free. Tin canny and cheap. The music poured out of the taverns, corny, tinny or jazzy, all mixing together with the sour milk, stale smell of the street. Kirk tightened up inside. He noticed his hands were shaking. The house he had built on hope might fall around his ears. He could feel the sweat under his shirt and his head was woozy.

When he picked Jeannie up late, he was drunk. She was tapping her foot impatiently as the cab slithered to the curb.

"Not again," she said.

Inside the cab Kirk ignored her questions. He was making decisions, and discounting them. Re-evaluating with a black gin-laden mind.

Up in the apartment she laid down the ultimatum.

"One more time." Acid in her words.

"Then what?" His tongue was thick but head clearing.

"I'm leaving—that's what," she ejected the words.

"Leave now, you exhibitionist bitch."

"That's all I take."

She was pulling the suitcase down from the closet when he hit her. Once, twice. Her muttered sounds. She sank to the floor, murmuring again. She locked her arms around his knees.

"No more. No more." Her voice was low, not angry. She held him tight.

Later in bed, lying close, their energy expended

and re-expended. He could feel the welts on her back
and her little exclamation as he moved his fingers
roughly across her smooth surface, hitting the relief
like an abrasive.

"Are you going to throw the letters away?"

"Yes, honey." Her voice parroted the answer.

"And no more of those films."

"Yes, sugar."

"No more talking about leaving?"

"No, honey."

"We go to New York?"

"Yes."

He drew her close. She whispered in his ear. "I
can't go to the *El Conejo* with these marks."

"Take some days off. We can go up to the zoo."

"To the zoo." And her teeth clamped his ear and
they rolled with the drunken turn of the earth,
conversing in Braille.

CHAPTER VIII

"May I see the bill again?" Jeannie asked.

Kirk watched her turn the phony ten in her hand.
A wrinkle cracked the smooth forehead. They had
spent the morning at the zoo. Now, just above the
border in Wisconsin, in a makeshift restaurant off the
highway, Kirk had given Jeannie the angle. Two
helpings of chicken had gone by the board and the
plump German woman cleared the dishes from the
table. Moisture beads formed on the ice-cold beer
glasses. Kirk puffed the cigar, and outside on the
highway a truck's motor grated as it went over the
small hill in the Windy City's direction. His eyes
returned to Jeannie. She pursed her lips.

"This looks as good as the real one." Jeannie

handed back the bill. "Still, it sounds risky."

"Not as risky as taking clothes off in a two-bit beer joint."

"I get paid."

"So do we."

"In hard cash?" Jeannie asked.

"Hard enough to buy the nine pair of shoes in your closet. Besides you're not taking any chances."

"I've heard that song before."

"Is the New York trip on?"

"This is a new twist. I want time."

"To see how the wind blows?"

"Yes." Jeannie smiled as she reached back to pat her rear. "What about the belt buckle?"

"Didn't we settle that?"

"New York isn't all. If things go right, who knows? We may end up in Europe."

"If things go right," she mimicked.

But Kirk knew the deal was half sold.

"I'll give you my answer tonight. Just watch the way you treat me."

Like a queen, Kirk said, mentally taking the words from Martin's line. Jeannie was getting cocky again, he noticed.

They stood up to leave and Kirk inquired about the washroom. He gave Jeannie a ten.

"Pay the woman," he said.

Outside in the rented car, the engine rumbled. Jeannie laid her head on his shoulder.

"Was that a good ten?"

"Good as the Statue of Liberty. Didn't you expect it to be?"

He knew the bill was as phony as the last bump from the runway. Phony as the baldheaded row in the conventions away from home. But the entire setup, Jeannie shoving the bill, was good for an angle when the chips were down. Jeannie would make the trip to New York, under persuasion if necessary. He shifted the gear and his hand rested on her knee.

The city was muggy and in the apartment Jeannie removed all her clothes. She moved toward the chair. In her hand she held the highball. Kirk settled in the couch, his bare toes gripping the carpet.

"Nice to spend an evening at home." From his position he could see the two bottles of whisky, the mix, and a big bowl of ice on the kitchen table.

Traffic, the distant elevated clatter, people's voices jabbering, were the hollow muted sounds of a background jungle. Jeannie's head tilted, listening. Her blonde hair was piled into a knot high on her head. Behind her two flies buzzed for position.

The cold drinks passed. Kirk lay on the couch, his head propped on a pillow. Sweat formed on his chest and beside the couch in a heap were his clothes. The room lights were out, and his mind twisted the liquor, molding it into shape. Jeannie re-entered the room from the kitchen. Without high heels she was short in the shadow of the doorway. In the subtle light her skin was like damask. She dropped to her knees beside the couch, her fingers curling his chest hair. She ran her lips along his neck, and her tongue stitched the previous night's anger, the hopes of more money and the dream of New York into a new reality.

When Kirk awoke, his hand caressed Jeannie's skin. She gurgled in her sleep. The absence of the usual Lake breeze caused the street outside to smolder in the heat. He adjusted his vision to the darkness. One more day of holiday at the race track and he would have to cut the mustard. Jeannie's welts were disappearing, and the manager of the *El Conejo* had called twice. The metal-processing convention was in town and Jeannie would work the weekend.

In the kitchen he slugged the whisky bottle twice, washed it down with the dissolved ice water from the bowl. Rummaging through the apartment he found one squashed cigar. Kirk worked his fingers on the accordion shape until it was an inch long. He rested his hands on the sill and watched the black empty street. After tomorrow, with Jeannie back on the job, he would dump bills fast and all day. Maybe he would work Gary. The streets were calculated and arranged from his memory. From the next apartment he heard a woman's voice.

"You son-of-a-bitch."

Bed springs creaked and that was all he heard. He turned his head attentively and the new heavy drops of rain hit the roof.

The track, big and spacious, was only a short safari from the city. The brassy-voiced selectors were hawking their cards.

"The clocker had the double," said the voice behind the green card. He waved the card in front of Kirk. "Two hundred nineteen dollar double, yesterday. Check with the clocker. Carry your loot home in a truck."

"Six in a row for the apex," said the voice behind the orange card.

Kirk and Jeannie walked through the selectors. Ten eyes followed Jeannie, and the five selectors nodded in unison. This was one filly that needed more than a straw bed. Kirk could hear their voices in the background. "I'd let that baby park her shoes under my bed any night," said the apex to the clocker.

And a big, raw-boned Negro in a candy-striped

shirt said, "That's right, that's right." He chuckled as he walked toward the clocker.

Jeannie moved through the turnstile, careful not to bump the bruises on her generous fanny.

Kirk purchased a racing form and they walked to the rail. Who the hell worked in the Windy City? Glancing up at the green-painted steel frames, and the swarm of people crawling over, back and under like ants, Kirk guessed that half the city was here. At least the half with larceny in their hearts. It was a confusion of color, faces and excitable talk. The something-for-nothing crowd, all dished up and sautéed in the pan of hope. The brilliant-shirted jockeys guided their frisky horses along the rail. The first race with the red-black uniformed trumpeter, blasting the *Come to the Post*. Layers of voices, calculations, predictions, and I know an owner, pressed the track into bedlam. Pressing tight into a watchspring that gathered fatigue.

Kirk selected four horses for the daily-double: two in the first race, two in the second, crisscrossing them. He purchased the four double tickets.

All the doubles missed. So did Kirk's selections in the third and fourth races. After the fifth, while walking up to the cashier's window with a fourteen-dollar ticket, he heard Martin yelling from a box.

"Kirk! Up here." Martin motioned to them.

In the box, Martin gave the introductions. "Jeannie, Kirk, meet the Egyptian." A heavy-set woman loaded with baubles turned from her seat. Under a turban hat, the sparkling jewelry conflicted with the deep-set, black-lined eyes. She acknowledged them with a quick wave of her hand.

"Sit down, sit down." Martin pointed to the seats.

"Order a pillow, will you, Kirk?" Jeannie asked.

"Someone bite you where it hurts?" asked Martin.

Kirk followed the neat pin-stripe suit up to a flushed tan face. Martin was loaded for bear with whisky. The chubby woman pardoned her way through them.

"Where did you find that, in an antique shop?" asked Kirk.

"Get this, brother. This is rich," Martin lowered his head, confidential-like.

"Been with her since yesterday. She's a madame. Has some joint down in Urbana near the university. Plays the college boys. Plenty dough. All that glass is real. I told her I was pimping out in L. A. Had a string of girls." Martin pointed his thumb toward Jeannie and laughed. "Said she was one."

"What!" Jeannie exploded.

"Don't get excited. We're going to pull the old girl's leg." Martin added, "Just say you're from L. A."

Kirk moved toward the opening. "I'm going to make a bet."

"Wait, I'll go with you." Kirk followed Martin. Martin turned back toward Jeannie. "Tell my honey about L. A."

Kirk placed his bet at the five-dollar-win window. He took his ticket on "Torrent."

"Look good to you, Kirk?" Martin asked, his face twisting into a grin. "Make it six on 'Torrent.'" Martin gave the man the number and threw three crumpled tens through the cage. "I have to hit the can," he said. "Did you notice the rocks on my baby?"

"Your baby's old enough to be your mother."

Inside the swinging doors of the urinal, Kirk saw a man leaning against the wall. His body dangled in space as if it were on a hook. The man had a face the color of week-old orange peels, his fedora was cocked crookedly on his head. His eyes were half-closed and his tie was sloppy. Under the opened shirt a triangle of hairy belly showed. He had leaked in his pants. So near and yet so far, thought Kirk.

The man coughed and the phlegm gurgled in his throat, and with every cough the wet area along his left pants leg grew larger.

Back in the box Kirk saw that the madame had Jeannie cornered. The madame's hands were fat, smooth and wrinkled. Bracelets ran up her arms, and there were rings on five of her ten fingers. The one on her left middle finger was a big diamond dome. Jewelry circled around her neck, tight, and her face set atop this like a cratered moon on a jeweled pyramid. To Kirk, one thing was certain. Business was awfully good in the college town. In her right hand she gripped her purse. Under the big dome dinner-ring on the left hand she had three one-hundred dollar tickets. The ends curled out of her fingers like the house man's currency in a crap game. This daughter of the Pharaoh was a big bettor, and her bet was not on "Torrent."

The madame's eyes rolled over Jeannie. Kirk knew her problem. College boys didn't want sacks. With all that young, good-looking stuff around the campus, competition was rough. After a long night of fraternity drinking, they would want a facsimile of the girl back home or the prom-queen. The madame was weighing Jeannie in for that trip down the Nile and the boat would never get to Little Egypt. In her eyes were mirrored the green bills that would hit the till every time Jeannie would leave the door open. The madame was concerned with Jeannie, and Kirk and Martin were concerned with the photo finish. "Torrent" came in second. The madame rose from her chair.

"I am going to cash these tickets." And then she said to Jeannie, "Powder your nose, dearie?"

Martin pushed Jeannie from her chair, and her hips looked small as she followed in the wake of the Egyptian barge.

"Get the girls acquainted," Martin explained to Kirk.

The horses from the last race were back in the paddock. Martin had flattened a fender on the Cadillac. It was being fixed. Kirk offered to drive Martin and the madame to their destination. The track looked like a big deserted barn. The afternoon's colors and honky-tonk atmosphere disappeared down the drain with the losers' tickets. The trash strewn along the concrete floor was carried into small mounds by a wind that whispered around the pillars. Lonesome losers' tickets whirled in spirals. Kirk led the way from the track.

The madame talked to Martin. Her tone was low and Kirk couldn't hear.

"The Egyptian wants to know if you're doing anything tonight?" Martin asked.

Kirk looked at Jeannie. She said, "I don't care."

"Why, what's cooking?" he asked.

"The Egyptian wants frog-legs and jazz music," Martin said.

And Kirk heard himself being talked into making it a foursome.

The frog-legs were cleaned to the bones, and the stomps and blues were embedded in the broken pavement around South State Street. The Egyptian was foggy on her own specialty, Sherry and Southern Comfort. It was after a high-yellow Lesbian dancer at the "Mable's Rest" made a pass at Jeannie that the madame suggested the group go up to her place for a nightcap. Her tone implied, we will make this a comfy party, just the four of us with no intruders. The madame was hot on the trail.

Her rooms were in one of the sportiest hotels overlooking the Lake. She explained her predicament while she shifted her eyes from Jeannie to Martin. Jeannie, sporting a big green orchid, listened.

"I come up to Chicago every year for my kicks," the madame said.

Kirk noticed that Martin was surprisingly sober. The whole relationship seemed fishy so Kirk had skipped drinks. The only glassy eye in the place was Jeannie. The madame's recuperative powers cut through the fog.

"Never discuss business with pleasure," said the madame. "But as I told honey boy, I do need a Number One girl. We have a nice trade. Only the best."

Jeannie nodded absently. There was a bottle of whisky on the table which Martin opened easily. Kirk went through the procedure of mixing the drinks. The madame disappeared into the bedroom and returned with four cigarettes in her opened palm. They were like the kind made in a Target rolling machine.

"Try these," she said.

Martin accepted one. He handed back the one meant for Kirk. "My friend goes bowwow on these." Martin winked to Kirk.

"None for me," Kirk said.

Martin lit his and the madame showed Jeannie the ropes. The three of them puffed and the liquor was left to Kirk.

Martin was higher than the pyramids. He waltzed on top with the Sphinx. Kirk didn't understand the cue completely; but he saw that Martin overplayed.

The madame was talking about the wonderful place. Kirk sipped the whisky. Jeannie was getting high.

She was standing in the room, the cigarette hanging from one corner of her mouth. She jiggled her body to imaginary rhythms, giggling after every step. Kirk looked at the madame. Her eyes were beady, moving up and down Jeannie's body. Maybe the madame was queer.

"My stomach has butterflies in it," Jeannie said, plunking herself into a chair. "Get me some ice cream, Kirk."

"Move, Kirk, you have a pregnant woman on your hands," said Martin.

Kirk watched the madame's ears wobble. "Not pregnant," he said. "Just wacky on that squirrel powder."

"Come on, honey." Jeannie's skirt was up, showing the flesh past the stockings. Kirk walked to the phone. He knew the bellhops in this place could get pheasant out of season. He ordered a quart of strawberry ice cream. He looked around. Jeannie and the madame were gone. Martin was tapping a finger on the table stand.

"Where they go, the can?"

"In there," Martin said.

Kirk pushed the bedroom door open. The madame was sitting on the bed, eyes open. Jeannie had her dress raised showing the legs up to her hips. She was pivoting around, giggling. The madame was appraising the body. Reaching up to caress the legs, touch the hips. Kirk said, "Out here for the ice cream. Save that leg showing for the *El Conejo*."

Jeannie fluffed out of the room. The madame got up. "Keep your crummy hands off her," Kirk said. He watched the madame grip her purse. Her body fell against his as she tried to move through the blocked door space. She was high too. Kirk's nostrils twitched at the creepy odor about her.

He sat down, watched Jeannie savor every spoonful of the ice cream, as if it were gold, and the shredded strawberries were rubies. He would have to knock off drinking. Another smoke of pot and Jeannie would end up in the madame's stable.

When the combination hit Jeannie, she went into a tailspin. The liquor, reefer and ice cream changed the tan face to a ghastly green. Kirk guided her to the bathroom. She was on her knees, gripping the bowl. He held her hair back to keep it clear of the water. Her insides rattled and the water spun in the bowl. Her wilted orchid followed the mess down with the flush. Kirk heard a loud thud from the adjacent room. He helped Jeannie to her feet.

"Can you make it to the car?" he asked.

Her face was still pale and she nodded weakly. Outside the bathroom Martin was pocketing a short, stubby thirty-two revolver.

"We have to go," Martin said. There was no trace of the pot in his actions. The madame lay flat on the floor, her two stocky legs protruding from the bedroom. Martin used one foot and pushed her legs into the bedroom's darkness. On the floor near the table the madame's purse lay opened. Martin hurried them from the apartment. He tipped the elevator boy a dollar. The revolver had been the madame's protection; but in the excitement of Jeannie's vomiting, the madame became careless. She had turned her head and one well-placed rabbit punch had done the trick.

"We couldn't allow her to take our little girl. Could we, Kirk?"

Kirk drove in silence and Martin playfully patted the inert Jeannie on her rump. On Woodlawn Avenue no one was out to see Kirk carry Jeannie into the apartment entrance for the second time in one month.

In three days of operation he passed over one hundred bills. His main problem was consistency. In the last week his relationship with Jeannie had improved.

Kirk had a routine established. Pass the phonies all day and then he would have a big meal with Jeannie. Then she would go to the club and after several hours of sleep he would come down for the last strip. Sometimes they would go to sleep early, which meant five in the morning. Often Jeannie greased the slides under his schedule. All these things reflected in his mind as he entered the next place.

The liquor store was long and narrow. Kirk walked toward the counter which was set in front of the icebox at the extreme end of the store. He moved toward the cigars near the cash register. When he turned to pay, the proprietor was up in front dealing with a customer. Kirk's eye went to the small card pasted below the register. He moved closer, toyed with two packages of gum. Straining his eyes, Kirk discerned the number. Premonition had rung the bell and he was right. There were two series of numbers and they were from Martin's plant, wherever it was. The owner moved toward the counter. Kirk fished a half-dollar from his pocket and paid for the gum and cigars.

Over in the old neighborhood, behind the stockyards, Kirk worked Morgan Street. Owners of the shops, beer joints, shoe stores were foreigners. These people were not savvy in the phony-bill department. In Europe, the marks, kopeks, lires and francs fluctuated with the irregularity of a badly tuned heart. A small change in government and the money values would go from luxury to zero. People would grumble and accept the new exchange rate. But this was for Europe, the old country. In America, all money was backed by the gold buried deep in American steel and concrete vaults. There foreign born were shrewd in some ways, too trusting in others. Kirk passed seven phonies in twenty minutes.

In an hour he moved down Archer Avenue near Halsted Street. This street would be good for the remainder of the day. He had only twenty phonies left. Dump them today and he would be ahead of the game. He could sleep late tomorrow while Martin went for another stack. In the next block, he pulled the Ford from the curb and surveyed the back area in the rear-view mirror. Another car with two men in it pulled behind him. He stopped the car at the corner, the car behind rubbed his bumper. The two men were talking. Kirk concentrated on their lip movements in the mirror. The men were nonchalant, as Treasury men would be, sure of themselves, not easy to fluster. Kirk jammed the Ford into gear and moved around the corner. The other car turned with him. For three blocks he held the wheel with one hand and assembled his last three bills into the other hand. Slowing down, but still watching the following car, he allowed the wheel to guide and rolled the three bills into a knot. When he turned into an alleyway he casually threw the money from the window. Goodbye evidence, he thought. At the far end of the alley he looked back. There was nothing in the mirror but one alley loaded with garbage cans. A golden stirring went through his mind. Backtrack three blocks and he found no trace of the other car. His tail was only a figment of imagination. He drove toward the alley.

Two small boys were playing near his spot when he stopped the car. He got out and left the door open.

"Watcha looking for, mister?" said one tousled head.

"A hub cap. See any?"

The two boys started to look, so did Kirk. The broken bottles reflected the sun. The garbage cans were uncovered, odors of rotten cabbage and fish heads, soft mush orange smells exuded from them. Near a broken down fence Kirk found the money. He placed it in his coat pocket and dusted his pants with his hands as he approached the boys.

"Didn't find no hub cap, mister?"

Kirk said, "Forget it."

He extended his hand and gave them each a dime. They watched him as he gunned through the remainder of the alley.

He parked the car on the east side of the Illinois Central viaduct when he came to Sixty-third Street. He waited for a break in the traffic to cross to the poolroom. Maybe he would have a quick game with Barney.

Barney was at the rear table playing with Martin. Barney cued his stick and a carefully executed bank shot moved rapidly into the side pocket. Martin moved his cue when Barney missed the next shot.

"Seen Doyle?" Kirk asked.

"Not this week. Maybe he's sick like Jake," Barney said.

"Jake sick. I thought he was at school. From what?"

"Had his appendix removed, so he came home. Why don't you visit him? Cheer him up." Barney said. Kirk watched Barney gauge the coming shot.

"How did the afternoon go?" asked Martin.

"Over forty bills."

"Good, kid, good," said Martin.

"Pickup tomorrow?"

Martin missed his shot, an easy one, the ball rimmed the cup.

"I won't until next week. But I have you covered."

Kirk looked at the tie. He saw the diamond glass-domed dinner ring of the madame's. It was set in a stickpin and the stickpin was in Martin's tie. It was obvious. Martin had arranged the entire evening. Using Jeannie as a lure he had sucked in the madame. Sucked her down the creek for bankroll, rings and gun. If the madame squawked they would all be in the pokey as a three-party roll job. But who had the loot? Martin. Kirk walked out the door.

Jake was wrapped in a cotton bathrobe. Kirk sat across from him and moved the ashtray stand near. He could see Jake's bare legs and the big bedroom slippers.

"What happened?" he said.

"Nothing. Just the appendix. I'm glad it came during summer."

Jake, with glasses on, looked like a professor, Kirk thought. A big man going in a big direction.

"Any football at school?"

"Can't, Kirk. Too hard to mix with the harvesting."

"You bastard. I can see you now. Wheeling a big Cadillac, Coach Jake the success boy."

"Look who's talking. Your suit cost more than my month's allowance."

"But the payoff is on the tail-end."

"I guess you're right, Kirk."

"Jake, I'm neck deep in trouble. You know what I'm in."

"Everyone on Sixty-third does."

"It sounded easy at first. Make a bundle. Get a stake. Clear town. Maybe go down to New Orleans.

Now the dough goes out faster than it comes in."

"That's easy, Kirk. Get rid of Jeannie. Get a legitimate job."

"It's easy for you to talk, the old man's paying part of your freight." He saw Jake's forehead wrinkle into a frown. "I didn't mean it wrong, Jake." Kirk watched Jake's face. It was peaked. Deep circles under the eyes. His getting flustered over Jake's suggestions bothered him.

"Neither did I, Kirk. For your own good. Get out of the racket before you end up in Leavenworth. Dump Jeannie. Without her you wouldn't need all the money. You remember I always joked about tapping Jeannie, and how lucky you were? But since I've been away I heard about you two. Jeannie at the *El Conejo*. She's phony, Kirk. Phony as the made-up broads in the movies. They're for fruity people to worship, then go home to dream. Some kind of hollow dream. When you tie up with them everyone's trying to horn in. You're too close and get the wrong perspective. You think you have something special. Something everyone wants. Not everyone, Kirk. Just people on a kick. Jeannie's kind are a dime a dozen. Strip shows, hook shops, dance-halls, waitresses. Every dime-store in the country has two or three Jeannies. They're not special. Just a stereotype, and the goddam country's flooded with them. Junk her, Kirk, get wise."

"She has a full-length mirror. Parades in front of it, all day. Then she's like a kid in a candy shop, everything she sees, she wants."

"Dump her, Kirk. Jeannie will never be satisfied. She's like the rest. They end up carrying a mirror in the hearse with them on the last trip."

"But the one thing, in bed she's like a mink."

"She won't be a mink for you if you're doing time.

She isn't the kind that sticks. How about Martin?
Wasn't he hot for her frame?"

"He still is. They get chummier every day."

"Watch Marty," Jake said. "Remember what
happened on the bookie deal. The only one who took
the rap was you. Kirk, go down to New Orleans. You
always liked the town. Maybe you could get some
part-time job, re-enroll in Tulane. You're still young."

Kirk listened and he knew that Jake was right. His
stomach began to bother him, and he thought about
Jake as his long legs moved toward Woodlawn, his
thick hands gripped at his side.

CHAPTER IX

With Jake's advice still vibrating in his head, Kirk
entered the apartment, closing the door quietly. Kirk
heard the bubbling of water from the bathroom. He
was home unexpectedly; the room showed that
Jeannie's clothes were spilled around the room.
Moving softly, he opened the bedroom door.
Jeannie's trunk was open, and when Kirk lifted the
lid, he saw that the ribbon around the prize letters
was undone. Kirk fumbled for a match, then thought
about the cigar. He returned the matches to his
pocket. The water was still bubbling in the tub as he
crossed the room to kneel at the bathroom door. His
eye attached to the keyhole. Jeannie sat upright in the
tub, the bubble bath soap making foam higher than
the rim of the tub. A languorous smile played over
her lips and the towel wrapped around her head made
her look like a swami, the deep tan of her face almost
as dark as the Hindu girls. A chair faced the tub, and
as she puffed, fashioning weak smoke rings, her
tapered fingernails squashed the cigarette into the

tray. Kirk shifted his knee when Jeannie reached for the sheaf of pages. He watched the enraptured look and then heard the laughter as she went back to recheck a previous page. Jeannie at the pool of love, Kirk said to himself sarcastically. Jake had the situation pegged. Jake with his analytic mind, not the sloppy hit-and-miss thinking of gamblers, who relied on hope, luck tokens. He glued his eye closer to the keyhole, watching Jeannie place her finger to the curve and contour of her lip, slowly tracing the lip outline. She put the papers down, relaxing deep in the tub almost disappearing from view. Kirk's fingers shook as if detached from his body, controlled separately from the mind, the hands eager to go in and mash the languorous calm of the face. The pages were back in her hand and she read to the finish.

Kirk watched as she emerged from the tub, slowly as if enjoying every move. Now the scale and his eye followed the deep tan to the white albino area of the hips. Jeannie was made for a burlesque queen or to be a mother of twelve children, he thought. The body narrowed into her abnormally small waist and when she turned the upper portion of her body was out far from the body as if suspended. Nothing artificial about the erectness. And this resulted in the mixed feeling. Kirk heard Jake's voice in the background but up close, this close, the fingers changed from the desire to rough up that frame, to a feeling of caress. The urge to slam open the door and carry her into the bedroom was switched when he thought about the letter. Jeannie had the sheer black nightgown over her shoulders, the towel still wrapped around her head. She picked up the letter and as her feet slid into the mules, Kirk moved swiftly from the room.

When Kirk entered the *El Conejo*, he saw Martin

piled high and deep, sitting with Jeannie, their heads almost together, and talking. The pink-gold of Jeannie's hair was changed again, back to the natural deep-carbon brown. This was the reason for the swami towel today. As she bent over, deeply engrossed in the conversation, the heavy waves of hair touched the table. The M. C. was listing the celebrities or what passed for celebrities in the *El Conejo*. "Judge So and So," and some goony wizened twist in an orange papier-mâché hat, would get up to take a bow among the catcalls. "Bring on the girls." Place packed, every bar stool, every table. No wonder Jeannie picked up two hundred a week, and Kirk remembered Jake's words. Jeannie was queer for Paris labels. The reason her amount didn't always get into the kitty. Pushing his way through the remaining group he dropped heavily into one of the chairs. Jeannie's hand stole over his.

"You're late, honey," Jeannie said cautiously.

"Went to see my fortune-teller."

"What did he say?" asked Martin.

"That I'm going to get a letter, a nice long letter." But this was lost on Jeannie and Martin. She was leaving for the dressing room, a trail of expensive perfume erupting in her wake, and Martin was heading for the can.

Lots of guys would wonder, he told himself, how a guy could sit and watch four hundred people mentally manhandling his girl, out in the center of the floor in her birthday suit. In a way he was proud, proud of the envy and hopefulness. Self-satisfied in knowing she would fulfill any excitement she aroused in him. In another way he knew Jeannie was as phony as the bills he shoved. This side of him was fed up with money, Jeannie, rackets, angles; but it didn't have control. He thought about his getting sore two weeks ago when Martin was in their rooms. Jeannie walking out of the bedroom in pants alone with Martin sitting, eyes lolling like a nanny goat. Marty could see as much if not more here; but that was on a personal level.

"Ever see a joint this jammed?" Martin was back, he moved close to Kirk. "How did Jeannie find out about the bills?"

"She found the can, the coffee-ground can. Besides, she's been out with me in the afternoon. Marty, she's wise. She can put two and two together. She knows I'm no Midas."

"How long has she known?"

"Two weeks. I've been buying her clothes and baubles with the stuff since then. That makes her an accomplice. Doesn't it?"

Their attention was diverted to the stage. Their table was in the second tier. Clear view. The smoke circled and washed the lights. The brilliant center one, illuminating the stage like a lineup.

Red-headed M. C., short and corny, was reaching for them tonight, doing his feature, "The Ace in the Hole." Straw-hat stuff for the old-timers. Kirk noticed the edging forward in the chairs when Jeannie's number was announced.

"Built like a brick shipyard. Our importation from gay Paree. Miss Sex herself, the one and only Jeannie, doing her newest novelty: A day at the amusement park." During the applause the M. C. moved the microphone from the stage and all eyes were on the red-paneled dressing-room door.

Jeannie entered the stage, moving languorously, and lasciviously, almost busting out of her loose-skirted gold lame dress. No stockings on the saffron-tanned legs. Not too much makeup. She didn't need any—the load of massed brown hair, the

high-relief figure. Variation on a single theme ...
stroke the audience, caress them, blow them up like
balloons, mirror into their waiting eyes. She paused
before the red velour curtain, illuminated in the hard
brutal light. Her index finger was poised under her
chin, coy and girlish. Suddenly an air-hole vent
billowed the loose gold lame skirt exposing the
magnificent thighs. Prancing around the stage,
Jeannie leaped over the air vent, her hands attempting
to hold the flapping skirt.

Kirk saw the light gradually dim, leaving only the
twisting, sinuous silhouette of Jeannie, and behind her
the enlarged duplicate shadow on the red velour
curtain. The light glowed, enlarging to encompass the
large center of the stage, Jeannie's dress fell, to leave
the two-toned body nude, when the red-velour
curtain parted. More circus music, as Kirk became
conscious of the oversized fun-house mirror behind
Jeannie. The two figures danced, one faced forward,
the cushiony hips, the narrow waist, and the bursting
breasts, pink tipped as a white rabbit's eye; and the
other in the fun-house mirror, the jiggling pachyderm
hips, and the elephantine amplitude of her body,
rolling like jello. A bonbon fat bouncing ball
imitating in reverse the squirming antics of Jeannie.
Jeannie bounced and the gigantic jellowy two-toned
proportions repeated in the mirror. Sweet notes on
the trumpet saying, "The girl with the Plexiglas hips."
The audience responding, curtain closing and the light
narrowing on the lovely, fat, squirming belly that met
Broadway half-way. Kirk caught her wink as she
kicked her leg at the audience, all in one movement at
the exit.

Martin clamped him on the shoulder. "You lucky
bastard," he said.

Kirk saw the oily suave manager walk into the

dressing room, and when Jeannie didn't appear, he crossed the floor and entered.

The manager, his highly polished, patent-leather shoes turned inward like some pigeon-toed freak, stood trembling.

"What did our contract say?" The manager tapped his toe almost girlishly. "What did it say?"

Jeannie applied her lipstick carefully, pretending not to hear. He had the contract in his hand. Kirk could see that neither Jeannie nor the manager was aware of his entrance.

"It says you are to be here on time for six full shows. You were late tonight, and two times last week. Two hundred dollars a week is not hay. And most important you were to be a blonde. How many times have I said, that the headliner in this neighborhood must be a blonde. Are you listening?"

"Yeh! I can hear you, so can half the street," Jeannie said. "Oh, Kirk."

The manager pushed the contract under his nose. "Read it to your woman. She must be a blonde, or she gets second billing. We bring in another girl."

"Take it easy, hotshot. Jeannie's packing the house. What do you want?"

He stamped his foot. "Either she changes her hair or she gets second billing."

Jeannie's voice was incisive and bitter. "Get this into your oily head. I'm not bleaching my hair again, and there will be no second billing for this little girl."

"Then you're through. Through. Through."

"Do you think this upholstered barn is the only place I can work? You can get someone to fill my bill right now, see how your customers like that."

The manager stormed from the dressing-room and Jeannie raked all her gowns to one side, laying them carefully on the dressing table. "Go tell Marty to pull

the Cadillac around the back. Honey," her hands
toyed with his neck. "We can stop for a big stiff
drink."

They had steaks at the "Bamboo," saw the
floorshow at the "Chez Paree," listened to Muggsy
Spanier's fluted lips hit the oldies, and now deep in
the night sipped their drinks at the "Rabelais." Kirk
glanced from the amber-filled ounce glass to the
old-fashioned glass of Marty's and over to the sedate
Stinger of Jeannie's. He allowed his eye to linger over
the careless uncovered nyloned knee of Jeannie. How
had he allowed Martin to steer Jeannie to the
"Rabelais"? He searched his mind for any difference
in Martin's behavior. He speculated on the long
dance at the "Bamboo," Martin and Jeannie for three
long songs, and never close to the table. Only
occasionally could he catch their bobbing heads.
Kirk's fingers tapped the table.

"Nervous from the service," Martin said. Jeannie
giggled.

"Why don't we call it quits," Kirk said.

"Celebration," Jeannie inserted. "Celebration for
a little girl who will no longer show her frame."

Some sweatered college kid stood twinkling eyed
and asked Jeannie for a dance. "Beat it," Martin said.

Another round of drinks and Jeannie giggling
again. "Where did those sticks come from at the
madame's?"

"Why?" asked Martin.

"This little girl could go the hip-swinging route."

"They can be had," Martin said. "Any time, any
place."

"Don't be a chump. Come home and get some
sleep," Kirk said.

Jeannie leaned toward Martin, her hand on his
sleeve. "Kirk doesn't want any fun." She giggled

again.

"Fun! Christ, you were so high the other night, you couldn't hit your can with either hand."

The early pang of jealousy over Jeannie's behavior was replaced by a plan. In the hidden recesses of Kirk's brain was a small buzz of what could be Jake's warning. Go to New Orleans. He began to feel a control over his destiny. A quiver of anticipation ran through his body. Another whisky slipped down his throat like an amusement park coaster on its track.

"Hollow leg?" Martin asked. But Kirk sensed this was idle conversation. He hadn't buddied with Martin for fifteen years for nothing. Martin had a one-track mind. Jeannie was on that track. One string end cigarette would make it a one-way trolley. Beads of sweat formed on Kirk's upper lip. Inside, he was weary, shots of light flashing behind his eyes. A panicky feeling to get away from his cat and mouse game. Martin would get no virgin. He hadn't. Why endanger himself for the Federal rap? Martin taking it like a sultan, while he was breaking his prat to keep Jeannie comfortable. Now or never a small voice said.

"I'm going home. Are you coming, Jeannie?"

A small round circle of silence seemed to set their table away from the hubbub of the "Rabelais." Jeannie had stopped her irritating giggle.

"Are you coming?" Kirk's voice was bitter and caustic. Now or never, a voice said. Across the table, Martin's face was pale.

"Sure, Kirk. We all should call it quits," Martin said, and the impending tension and choice were relieved.

Kirk followed Jeannie up the stairs, and the Cadillac, snaky and smooth on the precisioned cylinders, ripped along the outer drive. No one said a word and the high trees of Jackson Park were blue green in the incandescent street lights.

When Kirk opened the door of the apartment the first streaks of dawn entered therein. He poured a drink from the fresh bottle and sat across from Jeannie as she, sullen and tipsy, removed the paisley blouse. Shafts of morning light glistened on her shoulders. And as the brassiere fell to the floor a wave of drunkenness rotated in his veins. He could sense the heart pulse under the large erect breasts. Her skirt preceded the band and buckles that held the sheer nylon. Crossing the room, he pressed his body against her but the struggling was too much. This was like an attack. He released her to look at the blood-red pout of the mouth. He couldn't force the effort, too much trouble in one day. He listened to the soft bare pad of Jeannie's feet as she went into the bedroom. Outside, the morning traffic was beginning.

The bottle was almost empty and Kirk sat watching the beams of sun cross-section the room like the scroll and lattice work of a New Orleans' fence. Kirk sat, immobile and impassive, grinding his third cigar into the tray. One beam of light touching Jeannie's open purse, only momentarily, just enough for Kirk to recognize the white tip of an envelope.

Checking the two dates of the envelopes, Kirk saw the September 25, 1951. Two days ago. Possibly the letter Jeannie had in the tub this afternoon. And one dated yesterday. Both addressed to the *El Conejo*. Tossing the envelopes on the couch, he crossed into the bedroom.

Jeannie lay nude, her arms apart, a thin sliver of sweat between her breasts. Leaning over her face, he caught the mixed odors of Moment Supreme, crème de menthe and brandy. He touched her arm. Jeannie stirred. "Don't, Marty," she muttered, and Kirk's eyes narrowed. Now or never the small inner voice said, coming back to haunt him.

One long finger twisted under the front-room rug, and Kirk pulled the one hundred eight dollars cached for future use. One more slug from the bottle, and he tiptoed to the bedroom. Jeannie had switched, and from his position the large thigh and haunch of the left leg seemed out of proportion. The clock on the mantel said nine o'clock. Kirk closed the apartment door quietly. He would satisfy one enigma before going to the station. Outside, he hailed a cab.

Kirk jumped from the cab and ran into the brownstone apartment house. Someone was cooking cabbage. On the third floor, he stopped by a room. He hesitated. His hand was up to knock. He pulled it down, and dropped to his knees. The keyhole was blocked by the key inside. The dim light from the room came through the transom. Kirk backed from the door, his moves cautious and silent. The transom was blocked partly by a rag. One area in the corner was ripped. He heard a kid banging on a pan below. With an easy move, his foot on the knob, his hand gripped the small ridge, between door and transom. By the tips of his fingers he pulled his face to the open spot. One eye glued to the glass.

The room was in disorder, papers strewn on the floor, a ragged floor mop propped against one wall. An odor of onion soup lurked at the transom. Kirk balanced on the knob, one arm propped against the jamb. He could see the green ink bottle spilled, staining a moth-eaten carpet; the bookcase loaded with heavy volumes, thick ones.

And around the walls, pictures of Jeannie pasted big and small like a cheap Rush Street art exhibit. All kinds of Jeannie and only of her. Bootleg ones from the camera club, that could be purchased in the cigar stores and shooting galleries. Under-the-counter stuff.

Others, bigger, stolen from the nightclub showcases. Evening gown pictures pasted unevenly along the walls. And in bed.

Doyle, naked, holding the plaster manikin. Kirk could see Doyle's face. He was sobbing, half in a trance, a sensual leer showing above his slobbering mouth. Now the expression changed, agony, as if someone had driven a silver stiletto between Doyle's ribs. Kirk could hear him say:

"Jeannie baby," and Doyle wrapped his arms around the manikin. The shades were drawn and only one naked long-corded light swinging.

Kirk dropped to the floor. He turned the knob quietly, but the door was locked. He pounded on the door. There was silence, a long silence that moved into the hall and seemed to have weight. It pressed against Kirk, his stomach was tightening. His legs felt weak and then strong again. His feelings indecisive, from anger to amazement.

"Who is it?"

"Telegram."

Doyle swung the door inward about an inch and Kirk pushed it open with his foot. Doyle backed away. His eyes open, mouth twittering with terror. Kirk closed the door behind him. He looked from the pictures to the manikin to Doyle. Doyle had the sheet in front of him. With nervous moves he was trying to cover up. Doyle with the sheet on looked like a Roman Senator or someone going into a Turkish bath.

Kirk walked toward the table. His big hand closed on some pages, a letter in progress. His other hand was at his side, the long arm limp and hand pointed downward was almost at his knees. He looked at the sheet.

Doyle was clutching him, struggling with him,

trying to grab the pages. Kirk pushed and Doyle fell on the bed. He was back up, sitting, a queer look on his face, the eyes without glasses were watering. He watched Kirk's clenched fist. Moved back to Kirk's face again.

"Don't, don't," he sobbed. Kirk crushed the pages in his hand. They dropped to the floor. Doyle was on his knees. Kirk could feel Doyle's head against his thigh. The body was shaking with sobs; he could hear Doyle crying.

With the right hand, he reached down and patted Doyle's head.

"You poor, miserable son-of-a-bitch."

Kirk closed the door quietly behind him. He could still hear Doyle's sob, and he was almost down to the first floor before the sobs stopped.

The Dixie Express left the Union Station at three-fifteen. Kirk sat on the inner seat, a *Life* magazine open on his knees. The silver blue train moved smoothly, hardly more than a steady click as it rolled over the rails. The dirty tenements clicked by the windows like dusty soldiers falling back in short order drill. Some gandy-dancers were driving spikes on a side rail. One workman with a moustache waved at the train. Kirk gave a feeble answer. When he passed Sixty-third Street, Kirk had a pang deep in his heart. The anxiety to leave, now alternating with doubts. Had Martin and Jeannie circled into one orbit, or had the distrustful stain of three years in prison conjured something untrue. By the time the Lamont quarries spun by the windows, Kirk was headed to the club car. He knew two stiff drinks would cancel any feeling.

The club car was crowded, businessmen, salesmen, and what looked like a honeymoon couple near the bar. Kirk sat at the small circular tan-leather bar locking his foot in the aluminum rung.

"What do you use for bar whisky?" he asked the bartender. The florid Irish face broke into a smile, and the meaty hands reached for the bottle.

"Seagram's Seven," he answered.

And as Kirk tilted the glass, he was hardly conscious of the young anemic man who lifted to the seat beside him.

"Good town, Chi," the anemic young man said as the train sped over the rolling green hills. "Good gambling town."

"Yeh," said Kirk and he ordered another. "Give one to Lucky." He jerked his thumb to the young man.

A few more miles and he would be farther away from Chicago than he had been in six years.

"How far you going?" asked anemic.

"All the way."

"New Orleans?"

"Yeh, why?"

"Give my friend a drink.... No, better than that ... Bushmill's," the anemic young man said.

By the sixth drink, and forty clicks past Spring Valley, the front was dropped.

The anemic blond man was standing ready to leave. The pasty face, centered between the padded shoulders.

"New Orleans is a long way. A few of the boys are getting together, nothing professional. A friendly game. The men's room of car seven." And to Kirk he was the pimp in all the doorways, the patsy at the sideshows, the shill over the green baize tables, the kid with the cue in every gold spittooned poolroom, but most of all the blood brother of every bill changer in the girlie machine circuit. The bloodless lips barely moved. "If you feel lucky, the cubes roll at eight."

CHAPTER X

Crowded and smoky, the men's room of car seven seemed to be the train's center. All the fast talkers on the train were cramped into the room. Some drunk, their eyes on the ever-diminishing circle and ever-changing bankrolls. The cubes bounced against the backboard, and they tinkled in Kirk's head like ice cubes in a tall *El Conejo* glass.

He followed the roll of the dice mentally calculating the bets and side bets. He was soberer than most, and still had forty-five dollars left.

Kirk made one side bet, then others back and forth until the cigar smoke thickened. Eighter from Decatur. Little Joe from Kokomo. Box-cars and two big sixes came up and back around. Kirk was down to twenty-eight dollars when his turn came. Kirk scooped up the dice, feeling the heat in the long used cubes. Maybe his luck was due to change. He needed a change. No chance of entering the sea-food town without cash. He thought of the New Orleans newspaper he had purchased at the Springfield stop. Waterfront strike. Ships tied up. Thirty-eight thousand idle. This was the test.

Placing a ten on the floor, Kirk rattled the dice. The long arm shot out, fingers snapping. Two solitary black dots.

"Snake eyes," someone said.

Kirk threw another ten.

"Cover it," and Kirk watched the anemic blond man, down on his knees, adjusting the bets. Along the wall, the spectators, losers or yet to get in people, leaning forward to catch the bounce of the cubes.

"Faded. Roll." The anemic man motioned to Kirk. Once again the rattle and coaxing chatter.

"Be nice to papa." Kirk cajoled for his point.

Box-cars. Six and six, big as day. Two crapouts in two rolls. Two flops in two tries.

"Any more?" said the anemic man.

"Roll, or get off the pot," said the hatchet-faced man who had the window seat next to Kirk's in his car. "Separate the men from the boys."

Kirk tossed the remaining eight dollars on the floor. Easy this time, one roll, a six and a lazy flop ace. Sixteen dollars.

"Let it ride," said Kirk caressing the dice. Fingers slipped over the polished cubes. The closest in the circle knelt, others stood behind. Some were on the seats stretching their eyes. No neutrals here. Eyes on the dice, wishful eyes that would follow the cubes to the backboards and watch the bounce. Kirk saw his arm outstretched like something detached from his body and the big thick fingers springboard the dice into the smoke and alien eyes. They hit the backboard, turning into a pair of deuces.

"Deuces never loses," he said.

He rattled the dice, sweat pouring down his neck, soaking the shirt. When the dice bounced, all eyes glued on the nine.

Once more. Why did I ever leave home, the rails sang. Kirk hesitated, then another long roll and the bounce. Five and two. Seven.

He was replaced by another, who would do the ballyhoo, roll the hoopla. Kirk walked back to the chair seat. Chilled now in the spots where the sweat had wet his shirt. His fingers fumbled for the last cigar and before he could light it, exhaustion overtook him, sinking his body deep in the outside seat.

"In your face," someone mumbled in the car.

In your face. The words mixed with the sultry air, worked around Kirk's ear and drifted into his dream world with him. It was twilight, and the spring rain had stopped, allowing the car tires to slap and hum away. Jeannie in pink organdy. Jazzy music, and she moved that compact rear like one of the freight trucks backing into its stall on Water Street. Jeannie's small teeth and those big thick lips.

"I'm gonna ketch—I'm gonna ketcha." Blue lights, one lost blind man and a musty cellar with imported wines and nine-inch cigars just off the Cuban boat. The jockeys high in their seats and the rotating navels on Clark Street. Jeannie's lips a crimson red oval and growing bigger, ready to swallow. The teeth—snap.

Kirk watched the whirring darkness when he awoke. The engineer was highballing the Big Jack over the dusky landscape. The conductor was coming through.

"What stop is next?"

"Cairo. Ten minutes,"

Kirk sat impatient and nervous. Broke. The one hundred and eight dollars in Chicago had dwindled to a round zero. He had been on the merry-go-round for three months. Three months in a never-ending circle. Grabbing for the gold ring had been futile. Silver-blue Dixie Express whipping through the night like a racetrack whippet. Kirk inadvertently brushed his elbow against the other passenger. In the dim light, he saw the hatchet-face. The Big Shot. The big bettor was sound asleep, buzzing the compartment with a buzzing snore. Kirk fumbled with the cigar, the smoke was sultry. He tried to shut his eyes and feel the smoke, but it was like puffing air. Opening his eyes, he saw the cloud of puffed smoke. Money, that was the answer.

Kirk thought, to enter New Orleans broke was impossible. Chicago, Chicago, said the creaking train. His destiny was not in the South, but back in the Windy City. What would Martin and Jeannie be doing? Would they be puzzled and worried over his disappearance? Or would they think about him at all? The train lurched and his body bumped into hatchet-face. The snores kept on. Kirk looked in the dim blue light, straining his eyes. The man's suit coat had draped aside. The inner pocket was exposed. Kirk could see some envelopes. When he looked closer, he saw the edge of a brown wallet, the kind that opened like a book. Turning in his seat he surveyed the passengers. No one was moving. A few minutes from Cairo. Kirk itched under his collar, and again the feeling he had when watching his horse come down the stretch rumbled through his body. The man stirred, his arm covering the vital inner pocket. Kirk knew this was his last chance to go back. Leaning his face close to the other's.

"We're coming into Cairo," he murmured into the man's ear.

No reaction.

Kirk prepared himself on the next lurch. Placing his fingers at the edge of the coat. Time long. The train was slowing down. He heard the conductor again.

"Cairo. Three-minute stop."

The lurch. A small one, not as big as expected. The fingers prowled into the coat, as his shoulder shoved against hatchet-face's shoulder. The fingers fumbled, catching the wallet. The man was stirring, as Kirk pushed the wallet into his own inner pocket. The air brakes sizzled and Kirk stood, looking down at the man. No snores, but it would take at least a few minutes for his mind to activate. Kirk hurried to the exit, and leaped from the train as it came to a stop.

Hurrying along the long-boarded platform, Kirk leaped down the flight of steps. Walking, walking under the empty vastness of the sky. The street light placed the buildings into blocky shadows. In the distance, he heard the train whistle. The Dixie Express was on the move. Somewhere at the edge of the ominous river, Kirk sat among the reeds. A cricket chirped. Kirk lit the butt, sucking heavy on the soggy cigar. The wallet was open and loaded with cards. Firm cards. Hatchet-face was a salesman. A big-shot salesman. A big gambling man. Separate the men from the boys. There was a ten and two singles. Twelve dollars in the empty vastness of the sky, by the Father of All Waters, the Mississippi. Kirk lay on the reeds. The moon appeared from behind a cloudbank. It was around midnight.

The sun warmed his face and a glint of light touched Kirk's opened eye. He turned to see the wallet, in his exhaustion he had forgotten to throw it into the river. Kirk sat up brushing the powerful hands through his crewcut, blond hair. He shook the twigs from his coat. Gimcrack, shambles, shacks. This was not the Gold Coast. Kirk saw an overalled man two blocks down. Placing the cards deep in his wallet, he wiped any prints from the leather with his handkerchief, then scaled the wallet into the river. Kirk followed its progress until the river possessed it.

Pushing his thighs along the road, for five blocks to the highway, Kirk saw the white shack. A neon sign said Jeb Porters. The sign was not lit. Elegiac music poured from the shack, and as Kirk came closer the distinct notes of *I Get the Blues When It Rains* came out to meet him. It was a Negro-combo. Delicatessen, liquor, breakfasts. One could place a bet, Kirk knew. Outside the window, he saw the stoplight. Breakfast and then the long trek back.

Kirk had pancakes, ham and eggs, and coffee, had never tasted this good. The chubby Negro woman bustled behind the counter.

"Many trucks on the road?"

"Jeb, man wants to know about trucks." The voice was high and crackly like.

The Negro was good-looking. The blue denim work shirt furnished a subtle contrast to the mahogany polish of the face. The man's hair was wavy, not kinky, with streaks of gray along the sideburns. A hybrid for sure, Kirk thought. Indian and Negro or some fancy mixture. The Negro's age was hard to determine, anywhere between forty and sixty. Kirk looked past him to the tobacco, rolled strips of Kentucky burley, can of snuff, roll your own, and one box of charcoal black cigars. There weren't any bands or wrappers on the cigars. At his left was the wine and whisky. Kirk saw the prices. Port, some unknown brand, twenty cents a pint.

"Plenty trucks. Catch them over that way." The finger long and crooked with a manicured fingernail that made Kirk think of an old Chinese mandarin.

"Could a guy drink wine in here?"

"What kind?" the Negro answered, combining the positive answer into a selling question.

"Some of that port."

Kirk sipped the port. It had a homemade flavor, almost licorice sweet. Dropping five nickels in the juke-box, he sipped the wine, occasionally exploring his mouth with a toothpick. Only seven in the morning. Yesterday same time he was in bed with Jeannie. And as the juke-box blared some of the earlier Goodman and Fats Waller's *Sweet Georgia Brown*, Kirk kept thinking of Jeannie and Martin. He would make a compromise. There was nothing he could do without money. Martin had the one-way conduit to the bills. Somehow he would get the money. If necessary, take Martin for a sleigh ride. Maybe go off with Jeannie alone. Or even go to New York and just disappear in the catacombs of the big town. He thought of the night on the reeds by the river. Contrasted that with the soft apartment bed and the cushiony exploring body of Jeannie. He jumped to his feet.

"Give me five cigars... How much?"

"Twenty-five cents." And the total bill was a dollar-ten. Things were certainly cheap in the river country of Illinois.

He hooked his finger at the trucks. Waited impatiently. Over a half hour and he was disgusted enough to walk. When the big Buick ground to a stop, the door flung open and a hail-hearty man with the face of a cherub motioned to Kirk.

"How far you going?" Kirk asked.

"To the Windy City." Kirk judged by his clothes, and the assured way the man tooled the car down the two-lane highway, that he was a salesman, a drummer.

"Any work in Chi?" Kirk said, to start a conversation.

"Work! If you can't make it in the Windy City, you can't make it anywhere." Kirk watched a wooden chute of the small cliff coal mine appear as the Buick rounded a curve. The car leaped like an arrow. He was on the way back, and fast along the highway, a stretched ribbon, like a fallopian tube, leading to the womb of the city.

CHAPTER XI

The salesman drove swiftly over the green-hilled landscape to enter the garden suburbs at the edge of the Windy City. Kirk lurched with the shifting motion of the car, listening to the tappets that needed adjustment.

"Driving a Buick is like carrying an orchestra with you," he said.

"Expect to dump it this trip," answered the laconic salesman.

They lapsed into silence again, as the wheels churned by the refineries with the tangled undergrowth of aluminum pipes and silver dollar tanks. The dry-rub dance hall floated past the window, and at the airport the salesman turned onto Sixty-third. To Kirk the city looked hard and cruel. Honky-tonk town, hicktown, frontiertown, spread out in a half moon along the shores of Lake Michigan. The pyramided structures of the downtown area centered and crammed between the interlaced neighborhoods. The Buick emerged from the railroad viaduct to race past White City, the discarded amusement park. The familiar territory and elevated tracks unfolded to Kirk like a vision from a discarded dream. He was back.

"Let me off at Woodlawn, the next stoplight. And thanks."

"Don't mention it. Glad the jalopy got us both home."

Kirk slammed the door quickly. Flicking his hand in departure as the light changed, and the Buick rambled, disappearing from his memory into the dust mote, stenciled shadows under the El tracks.

The apartment was empty. Dropping to his knees, he saw that Jeannie's luggage was still under the bed.

Pulling back the spread he saw that it had been freshly made. Possibly not slept in. The icepick sharp hands of the clock were at three and twelve. Half-way through the afternoon. The salesman had made the entire length of the state in seven hours. Kirk rumpled the drawers, Jeannie's expensive lingerie racked in neat and orderly. Dresses, jewelry all in place but the red-hot mink was gone. Kirk stood sucking his upper lip and clenching the big hands. Outside the beginning end of summer violated the air, bringing the Windy City into its own. He ran the chilled tips of his fingers over his chin. He needed a shave.

In the bathroom, he found the razor. Funny that during the previous day's excitement he had gone off without his prize possession. Kirk shaved swiftly, wiping the blade clean with a tissue. With the razor in his back pocket he hurried to the street. A quick whistle, and the cab made an illegal U turn to pull to the curb.

Martin's room was empty. No Cadillac outside, only the expensive clothes on the rack. Kirk crossed the room to the bed. Two dents in the pillow. He could see a lipstick stain on one pillow. Looking closer, he could tell if it was Jeannie or not. A faint scent of perfume wafted from the open window's breeze. His nose could not isolate the smell. Maybe Moment Supreme. Maybe something else. He tried again picking the pillow, pushing it against his nose. Maybe, maybe not, he could not be sure. Kirk hurried back to his own apartment on Woodlawn, walking this time, his long legs hurrying past the busy shops. He crossed the street to avoid Barney. Entering the apartment, he bounded up the stairs, to pause and wait outside the door.

He pushed the door open. The wide, expansive hips of Jeannie bent over the bed. She was over the bed pushing her unmentionables into the tan suitcase.

"Leaving town?"

Jeannie turned, the tanned face turning a ghostly white. Kirk could see the hand trembling. Jeannie interlaced her fingers together to control them. She fell back to sit on the bed. In the opened suitcase, he could see Doyle's letters packed in the corner. Kirk closed the door behind him, bracing his body against the door. Jeannie had on a black gabardine suit, a stylish black fringy slip peeking from under the skirt. Black heels and over her shoulders the heavy fluffy carbon hair. The color had come back into her face, the full nose shiny over the scarlet slash of her mouth.

"Leaving town?" He asked again, the words echoing from the hollow of the room.

"We all have to." She was calm again. Her fingers steady as she lit a cigarette. "Something up. Martin called. He's going to call back. We have to meet him some new place."

"We?"

"Sure. Where were you last night? Martin searched the bars. He didn't want you in trouble...." Jeannie exuded the purplish smoke. Standing to smother him at the door. Kirk's fingers twined in the thick hair. Tightening his fingers until the forehead pulled tight with the scalp. With the eyes shut, she had a distinct oriental look. "I was wild, worrying about you." Jeannie's words almost an inaudible whisper.

With one big hand he tilted her chin up, spreading the mouth. He felt the pressure go from light to heavy as the mouth sucked him in until stopped by the obstacle of the teeth. Give me Chicago, and one man-eating cannibal, his heart hammered. The whirring jangle of the phone interrupted him.

"That's Martin now," Jeannie said.

"Hello."

"Who? ... Kirk! For Christ's sake." Martin's preliminary hesitation turned to astonishment. "Where you been?"

"Safe."

"Have you been over to my place?"

"No," Kirk lied.

"Is Jeannie there?"

"Yes."

"Then get yourselves over to this address." Martin gave a hotel address on Fifty-fifth Street. "Go out the back way of your place. Walk down the alley until Sixtieth. Hail a cab but get out at Fifty-seventh and Dorchester. Now follow directions if you want to stay out of the pokey."

Kirk hustled Jeannie out the back door, her black suede heels gathering dust down the alley.

The word from Martin was a sledge-hammer through his plans, and the New York trip was sliding from his fingers. What would Jeannie do under pressure, with every Stage Door Johnny standing in orchids and Lincolns four deep?

Treasury men had clamped the plant. No more bills would be made and in Martin's words there was only one bright patch in this black melancholy smoke-ogre sky. Martin's pickup man had some bills but he was leaving town in a hurry.

"Did he say?" Kirk asked.

"He said no dice. Leaving town and taking all the loose stuff with him. I begged, but no dice." Martin was propped, his back against the dresser. Jeannie sat on the bed. Concern in her forehead. The black suit amply filled. Her eyes went from Kirk to Martin and the tongue wet her lips. Understanding in her eyes. She knew what Kirk said to himself. The town was clamped and no doubt they had been tailed. She knew the jig was up, and she would be an accomplice: every dress, rent bill, coat and essential spelled this out in big letters. This was a crisis and no minor one.

"What are you boys going to do?" She rose and straightened her coat as if to leave.

"Where you going?" Kirk said, gripping her arm tight enough to make her wince.

"Out of here."

"Why?"

"I'm not getting a prison suntan."

"Take it easy. No one's going in the pokey. Sit down," said Martin. Jeannie, released by Kirk, sat on the bed, her skirt over her knees. The long, full silk-stockinged legs were nervous and anxious.

"Tailed. We've been tailed. The Feds wouldn't be stupid enough to let us slip by," she said.

"Tailed, yes," said Martin. "But not here. My room is locked and so is your apartment. This room is safe. That's why I gave you directions. Making sure. No one knows we're here. Except the cockroaches and they're not talking. What the hell would you people do without me? This is nothing to be excited about. I was rocked for my roll Saturday at the track. Four thousand on one horse. Am I crying?" He addressed Kirk. "We have an out. We can't leave town flat." He pulled some bills out of his pocket. Pulled both pockets inside out. Letting this gesture speak for itself. "Kirk, are you in for the limit?"

Kirk looked to Jeannie. "How about you? Still leaving?"

She said, "Leaving town? We all have to. Don't we?"

"Have any money?"

"I'll throw in what I have. Not much. There's a couple hundred in the bank but I'm not going close to that place."

"That's right, Jeannie. No need to be excited. The account's probably covered. So we pool our dough and leave. Still, it won't take us far. Kirk, if we rush we can knock the pickup man."

Kirk nodded his head. "How?"

Martin pulled the madame's short .32 from his inner pocket. "The equalizer. Throw a scare, loosen him up, grab the money and leave."

Jeannie settled back on the bed. Kirk and Martin left. Marty stroked the Cadillac through the traffic.

They entered the alley. Going up the stairs, two flights. Kirk saw Martin ahead taking three steps at a time. "I hope he's still here," Martin said.

Their movements down the soft carpeted hallway were quiet. Door 3D. White enameled. Inside there were some movements. Martin gave the required knock. No movement inside. Martin knocked again, sharply with the same code.

"Who is it?" asked the voice inside.

"Martin."

The door opened three inches and Marty's gun was pointed between the widening eyes. "All the way, Jeff. No tricks." The door opened. Kirk frisked the older man. Gray hair, almost distinguished-looking. No gun. Martin's gun point directed the man to the bed.

"Ready to leave?"

"Marty, you'll never get away with this. The boys won't forget."

"The boys are leaving town like rats. All I asked for was one package, now it's all. Where is it?"

"What?" said the shy mouth and Kirk's left caught the jaw and teeth flush. Over the bed went Jeff.

Martin followed him over, gun pointing directly. "Talk, or the groundhogs will be delivering your breakfast. Where is it?" Jeff pointed to the dresser. Kirk ransacked the drawer. He came up with two packages between the shirts.

"We don't want to see your pin-money. Kirk!" Martin waved the gun.

Kirk spun the man around, threw a full fist into his bread basket. The man doubled and he straightened him with the left hand. Martin pulled his head forward by the tie. Face grimacing, Jeff tried to wrench loose. Kirk was down on the floor, face livid and angry. He wrenched the man's neck, gripping the lapel. "Talk!"

"You'll never get away."

"Jeff, my patience is getting short." Martin waved the gun. "Surer than Christ I'll put a bullet through you." Kirk followed Martin's rising anger.

Kirk ripping the bed sheet, a tourniquet around Jeff's neck. The old man was the worse for wear. One lapel was loose, his face red and blue, the gray hair scraggly and the tourniquet around his neck squeezing. His eyes were glassy. The mattress stuffing was out on the floor scattered. Hats, coats, suits. Suitcase. Martin's temper exploded. Kirk watched him kick the suitcase lock and the briefcase bounded across the floor, spilling packages of new bills on the floor.

Jeff fell forward exhausted. Dragging him by the coat neck, Kirk pulled him face forward and heaved him into the closet. Martin had the case closed and their steps were fast, down the hall. Running now down the steps. Kirk's nose caught the alley refuse, garbage smell, Lysol, that flooded the morning. Hurry home, baby, hurry home. Back to the Clark Street Nell Gwyn, the girl with the carbon-colored hair.

The bills were spread on the bed and Jeannie was smiling at the count, fluffing her hair at the back. Twenty-two thousand dollars. False, but good in-between money. Kirk could see her lips move into a petulant, sensual shape, a false mouth, part of an act. She was pleased, Cheshire cat eyes, purring and stroking the packages. Outside the Illinois Central rattled. Carrying the shoppers, women of leisure, men out of work, and what have you. We-don't-care people. People who slept well at night with rare emotions. Nice life, these mediocre people. Kirk guessed that they didn't have the troubles of three people in one broken-down hotel room with twenty-two packages of Alexanders.

"Kirk, one more job. We can't leave town without any real money," Martin said.

Kirk watched. Had Martin winked? He could feel the heartbeat, pounding, ready to jump from the shirt. He watched closer. Jeannie had thirty dollars in bills on the table. Martin only eight. Where was the madame's loot, or the big amounts Martin always carried? Kirk's nose twitched, he rubbed his fingers.

"How much will you go, Kirk?" Martin asked.

He looked across the table at Martin and Jeannie. Their shoulders were almost touching. It was as if he were the stranger, and they were together facing him. Pushing him into a squeeze play. His hand came up with change and it spilled on the table, some pieces rolling off.

"This isn't enough," Martin said.

Kirk watched him look at Jeannie.

"But the joint is hot," Kirk said.

Before he could continue, Martin interrupted. "What do you say, Jeannie?" She looked from Martin to Kirk's frowning face.

"Sounds right to me. If we dump some of these ..." Her long red-lacquered fingernails scraped the rubber band on one package. "We won't leave a trail."

It was all too pat, Kirk thought. Like being at a rehearsal where the shill sets up the square for the kill. This girl catches on fast. Her words sounded mechanical to his ears.

"Why can't we drop a few on the road? Enough for gas and food," he said.

"A trail like confetti. The Feds can follow us on the map. It's no good, Kirk. We have to shove some here, shove enough to clear us into New York."

Jeannie moved over to Kirk, leaned close to him. Rubbing her soft cheek against his sweaty cheek. Her finger trailed the back of his neck. "I think Martin's right."

"Kirk, in three hours we'll be heading out of town. The three of us. New York. Come on, Kirk, fifteen to twenty bills apiece and we will be on our way."

"Are you in, Jeannie?" he asked. Maybe he was jumpy, tightening up. His imagination running in circles.

"I have no choice and New York sounds mighty interesting to me. Anyway we'll be together and that's the important item, honey."

Kirk could feel himself weaken. And what other choice did he have? Going it alone would be no good. "Okay, give me the bills. Jeannie can go with me," Kirk said.

"Stupid. How's she going?"

"In the car."

"We can't rent any cars. Do you think they haven't covered our tracks? No rented cars. I'm going on foot. In fact, the jig's up, so I'll cover Fifty-fifth

Street. Dump at least fifteen, and twenty if you can. We can be back in two hours."

"And Jeannie stays here?" Kirk said.

"Sure, Honey."

Kirk looked at Jeannie. She had moved and now they were standing in a triangle around the table.

"Start moving, Martin," he said. "And everything will be square."

Martin went out the door. Kirk lingered behind. Jeannie's arms were around his neck and her telltale lips sprawled all over his. His fingers gripped her smooth Hottentot fanny. And the massaging fingers whispered of things to come.

Kirk whistled for the cab at the corner.

Kirk's second place gave no trouble; but inside he had a vague feeling. Unexplainable. Almost like a boy feeling brave in a Frankenstein movie; later, when alone, going home in the dark, shorn of the marquee lights, and the people seated behind the potted plants, the braveness replaced by a sense of uneasiness. It was midnight at three in the afternoon. His steps quickened, moving toward the corner cigar store. Thirteen more Alexanders to pass, thirteen more ducats curving into the future; and he would race back to the security of the Cadillac and Jeannie's arms. His mind grasped at the images: the talking mousetrap, gabby Martin and a tangible Kirk. Not one lost on the pavement, but one he could see, feel, hear, even crawl inside and guide down the revolving highway into the land of make-believe, skyscrapers, and New York Yankees. After thirteen more passes, Jeannie, the kid with the silk-encased hips, would be in the Waldorf. Kirk bumped into a plaster black-and-white Victrola dog outside a radio store.

The cigar store was crowded. Kirk forced his way

to the counter. He ordered two cigars and handed the ten to the clerk. The clerk's eyes met his.

"Anything smaller than this?"

Kirk fumbled into his pocket. He felt the change. "Can't you change it."

"Nope, look for yourself." The clerk motioned to the cash register.

Kirk extracted a mass of change. His fingers fumbled, two pennies dribbled to the floor. He handed the exact change to the clerk. One of the idlers pushed the two pennies toward him. Kirk could see the dice in the green roll-box. Snake eyes, the solitary dots said. He brushed the hand aside. When he left the store, a woman followed him. His winging arm movements brushed against his hip. He could feel the loose bounce of the razor on his hip. Reaching in, he touched the cold steel. A man came across the street. The face was familiar. Not a friend. Not from the neighborhood. Hell, no doubt it was someone he had met on a binge. Kirk turned into a stationery store, shoved one more ten. Three to go, he thought, and the man's face came back. It bothered him. Where had he seen it? Christ, am I jittery. The traffic on Sixty-third was heavy. The recurrent elevated trains clanked on the erector-set tracks. All the phonies out in force. An occasional bookie receipt ticket on the sidewalk. Then there would be two or three more. Finally a bevy splattered around a store, one of the neighborhood's many books. The morning headlines. All bookies closed. Maybe a few running underground. As usual, the newspapers were full of crap.

He stopped for a car while crossing Greenwood. Turning to look back, he saw a woman looking at a restaurant menu that was pasted outside on the glass window. Where had he seen her before? Back in the cigar store? Was his mind going fruit? Kirk, you need a vacation, it said.

The next store was a bakery. Empty. Maybe this was a chance for a quick deal. He entered the store and waited for the girl to appear from the back. More slow-poke help today. Everybody on a vacation. Slow-moving, like the traffic outside. No one in a hurry but Kirk. She came out of the back carrying a tray of doughnuts. She placed them carefully on the glass case. Someone else had entered the store.

"Give me some Long Johns," Kirk said. "Half a dozen."

The girl moved easily, her starched uniform crackling. She handled the Long Johns between her thumb and index finger. Listening to the drone of the fan above, Kirk's mind wasn't concentrating. Almost day-dreaming. He pushed the ten on the counter. Fingers gripped his arm. Kirk spun and he could see the extended wallet. Treasury Department badge.

"We want to talk to you."

"Screw you, mister." Kirk leaped, his fist hard. Everything he had drove along the curve of the forearm and the knuckles were the advance end of a projectile. The Treasury man fell against the glass counter. His arm moved to stop the fall, broke through the glass and the bloody hand squashed into the pastries.

Kirk was outside, running. He recognized the old woman and the parts assembled in place. He would have to break fast and lose the tails. No car, he said to himself. Quickly, he discounted making escape on foot. Good to hole up in the dark passageways tied to the alleys; but time discounted this. The newsie stand. A delivery pickup truck bulked big as day, with the driver standing one foot on the curb, the other on the pickup. The driver talking to the newsie. Motor

running in the pickup. Gas tank perched over the
hood. Kirk hurled the driver flat, he sprawled on the
sidewalk. Kirk inside the cab of the pickup now,
backing out. His hand jarred the shift, the gears
grating. Out and forward went the pickup truck,
Kirk's face pale, ghost-white, the muscled hands
locked to the wheel. He could feel one finger throb.
The swelling had started. Voices were shouting in
back. Through the rear-view mirror, he could see a
blue-coated officer.

The pickup moved down Ellis Street, black puffs
of smoke coming out of the exhaust. Kirk's plan
materialized, zigzag, cross the Midway at Woodlawn,
dump the pickup around Fifty-fifth Street. His vision
was clear. Never had he seen the day so bright.
Brilliant sun polishing the serrated towers of the
University with a cognac stain. Green grass on the
Midway like the chlorine water in the pools or the
diamond at Comiskey Park. The people were clothed
crabs scrambling on this green. The pickup moved
past the single grayblock stone of the stolid
Rockefeller Cathedral. The red brick frat buildings,
white-stepped, sitting solidly behind the front lawns.
Everything solid, bulky, steady but the pickup
whipped into a frenzy, dancing along the boulevard.
Pickup and driver fused into one, carried past the
hedges into a rat's maze with the escapes still open.

Kirk saw the alley at Fifty-sixth Street. The turn
would be sharp. His face almost ferret-like watching
the alley. His fingers ached. Gas pedal to the floor, he
turned. The rear-wheel traction shot him into the
alley, past the garages, cans, horse dung. The pickup
poured down, caroming like a steel ball, rolling for
the exit. He could hear the siren now, his hands
slippery with sweat. The pickup erratic. He would
have to get close to the hotel, shorten the distance he

would travel on foot. Time becoming more
important. Martin and Jeannie would be impatient,
waiting, anxious to leave. Martin and his ideas, pass
fifteen. If he had taken half the swag and Jeannie,
Martin could go to New York, but he and Jeannie
could have gone to California, land of milk and
honey. The pickup's tires squeaked around the
corner. Rubber leaving deep imprints in the asphalt.
Two more turns now and he would duck back into
the alley. He watched the Ford in the rear-view
mirror. Police on his tail. A shot whistled over his
head. Another, and its whine ended in a solid slap
against the pickup. Gas pedal down to the floor. Air
rushing by. Landscape changing fast. Brick buildings
dissolving sugar cubes in this race of time. One break.
All he needed was one break. Shake the police car.
Hightail it to the hotel. Blow town, but fast, never
this hot.

He could feel the heat from the overworked
motor, coming through the floorboards. And he saw
his out. An alley. The last one. He knew it. Turn fast.
Put on the brakes, go through a passageway, over the
fence would carry him into the street, hop, skip and
jump. Two quick blocks to the hotel. He gunned the
motor. Swerving around the corner to come to a
screaming stop. Quickly, he flipped a fence running
through the dim passageway, to emerge along a street
of elms. Crossing the street, he heard the echo of his
footsteps paddle behind him. His head throbbed.
Why had he taken a chance in that dice game. No
time for regrets, he cautioned himself as he staggered
down another gangway to emerge at the alley in back
of the hotel. His body brushed the rear fender of
Martin's Cadillac to enter the rear of the hotel.

He took his breath in quick gasps, trying to fill his
lungs with the much-needed oxygen. Pushing against

his thighs, one hand aching, Kirk came to the third floor to stop outside the door. Inside he could hear Jeannie's voice. Then Martin's.

"Hurry. Kirk'll be back."

Kirk shoved against the door to throw it open.

Jeannie stood with the suitcase in her hand. Martin was wiping lipstick from his mouth. Kirk looked to Jeannie's head, a velvet-jeweled-coronet, fitted, skull tight.

"A going-away gift," Kirk added. They faced him in amazement,

Kirk stepped across, pulling the velvet coronet from her hair.

"Baubles," he said. "Jeannie's a musical girl. She'll play in any flat."

"You don't understand," Martin said.

"Don't I?"

And suddenly the room was charged with terror. A sense of doom crushing against Kirk's head like the murky underwater crushing a diver's head into a broken eggshell. The odors of the city, all the beautiful girls in the after-work crowds in the Loop, the decorations at Field's during Christmas time with the carols, bell-ringing Santas. The smoky Indian summer, and yellow gold of the beaches. Awareness of what could be, the other orbit, the other circle of destiny. Somewhere he had entered the joyride, the something-for-nothing crowd; like a predestined animal he had prowled in the windy smoke-filled layers of the concrete jungle to become one of three depraved money-hungry gold seekers. Under the nembutal shades of night, three people had moved into elliptic channels that became smaller and more confining. To meet face to face at last with twenty-two thousand dollars in phony bills in a depraved room with walls thick as concrete. Watch

Martin, Jake had warned. The bad prison memories filled Kirk's veins and the smell of impending blood made him alert; until each movement in the room, the restless curtain, clogged his pores, itching and tickling his stomach.

Martin jerked for his pocket, and Kirk moved to jar the slender chin. He threw another fist, scraped Martin's jaw, to grab Martin as the gun skidded from Martin's grasp. His hands became enormous, out of proportion, muscled from every swing of the prison's sledge. Big hands gripped around Martin's throat and Kirk squeezed until the snap broke all energy from Martin's body. Kirk felt the body slip from his grip and across the room he saw Jeannie, the narrow orifice of the .32 blinking unerringly, and above the gun the brown smoldering eyes of Jeannie. The velvet coronet was on the floor, and in Jeannie's hand was the briefcase. Not her suitcase with the letters and clothes. No, the briefcase with the twenty-two thousand in phony bills. Kirk looked at Martin twisted crazily, the head lolling in an offset direction. Kirk glanced back at the .32. He was lying half a-straddle the couch, one hand behind his back touching the strip of cold steel from the side of the ivory handle. The razor.

"So, only two of us share," he said.

"Share what?" Jeannie's mouth forming the fishface oval.

"Money, Cadillac, New York."

"With you? You strangler. Every night when I went to sleep, those awful hands. They're abnormal."

"Like your breasts."

He had the razor clear of his pocket. Keep talking, he thought. Get up. Only get close. Get the gun.

On his feet he tottered.

"Don't come any closer," Jeannie said. She

avoided looking at Martin's body. "No closer," she threatened.

"At least give me half a chance to get out of town."

The razor was open. The cool steel chilled his hot trembling hands.

"No closer or I'll shoot."

Kirk leaped out to meet the muffled report in his hand as the razor slashed at Jeannie's face, a line, sparkling blood red from the upper cheek to the lip. With a clenched fist, he rabbit-punched her neck feeling the soft flesh give. Kirk was overwhelmed, momentarily. Streaks of pain shooting from his hand up his arm.

People had heard the report. Why was he so slow? The details were clear. The money and the Cadillac. Blow town. Bending to ruffle Martin's pocket for the Caddie's keys. The lopsided head flopping on a squashed neck. In the background. He could hear Jeannie like a voice in the distance searching for recognition.

"My face, my face. You've ruined my looks." Jeannie's voice a whine.

Where were the keys? Ruthlessly Kirk overturned Martin's body. He winced when touching the cold face.

"You *maniac!* You've ruined me." The voice a snarl.

Kirk ripped through Martin's side pocket to emerge with the keys in the aching bloody hand. A siren buzzing the streets. He had to make the car. Lose the headhunters in the city streets and streak out of town. He turned to see Jeannie on her knees, her eyes like shallow mudholes operating against the weak light. The gash, deeper than he thought. Blood dripping from her face. Miami tan gone, dissolved into a pallid zinc-white. Her hand was moving over the floor. Get out, his mind said. And Kirk reached for the briefcase. Inwardly he laughed. Sirens were converging into the near present. Keys, briefcase, his big fingers reached for the brass knob.

Explosion! Kirk's strong hand held the door knob as if it would separate from him, close the last avenue of escape. Fear shook his body. His jaw trembled. Where was Mom now? Explosion! And something alien twisting into his entrails, to make two matching holes to equal the one in his hand. Jeannie was sobbing, wild gasping sobs. A twisted city, broken escalator, and a gorgeous body suspended in nightclub smoke. Bubbles in an empty frame. Come back, it said, and his body fell from the door.

Kirk could feel consciousness slip from his fingers like silk from a stripteaser's leg. Now he heard a soft pat. Little feet, stealthy little feet scribbling his life along the carpet. He heard sounds and one screeching agonized laugh in the gray, suede, sputum, blood-veined, late afternoon. His arms and fingers were long again reaching for the tattered ragdoll as the last wave of darkness enveloped him.

THE END

George Joseph Benet was born in Chicago on May 27, 1918. He joined the Army just before WWII and served throughout the war. Afterwards, Benet moved to California where he married Camille Gage Morris, a rare book dealer in San Francisco. He then moved back East to Greenwich Village in 1952, where he wrote *The Hoodlums*, published under the pseudonym of John Eagle, selling a half a million copies. Later that decade Benet moved back to San Francisco, where he worked as a longshoreman and was a life-long member of the ILWU. He eventually got a masters from U.C. Berkeley and started writing again in the 1970s, producing two well-received works before he passed away on October 9, 1990.

Black Gat Books

Black Gat Books is a new line of mass market paperbacks introduced in 2015 by Stark House Press. New titles appear every three months, featuring the best in crime fiction reprints. Each book is size to 4.25" x 7", just like they used to be, and priced at $9.99. Collect them all.

Stark House Press

1315 H Street, Eureka, CA 95501 707-498-3135
griffinskye3@sbcglobal.net   www.starkhousepress.com
Available from your local bookstore or direct from the publisher.

Lightning Source UK Ltd.
Milton Keynes UK
UKHW022019110522
402841UK00009B/2327